the Toxic *Mistress*

Written By:

Gladys Stocks

The Toxic Mistress
Written By: Gladys Stocks
Edited By: Aaron C. Butler

ISBN: 9781967082711 (Paperback)
ISBN: 9781967082728 (eBook)

Library of Congress Control Number: 2025922392

Printed in the United States of America

BookButler Publishing Company
Upper Marlboro, MD 20774

TheBookButler.com

BookButler Publishing Company titles may be purchased in bulk for educational, business, fundraising, or sales promotional use. For information, please email:
info@thebookbutler.com

Table of Contents

Prologue..9

Chapter One
"Just Another Night"......................................11

Chapter Two
Mimosas & Mirrors..15

Chapter Three
Control Issues.. 21

Chapter Four
Unwanted Patterns.. 25

Chapter Five
Background Check 29

Chapter Six
The Brownstone..37

Chapter Seven
The Watchers 43

Chapter Eight

Unsettled Ground 47

Chapter Nine

Cracks in the Glass...53

Chapter Ten

Terms of Engagement 59

Chapter Eleven

Lines in the Sand...67

Chapter Thirteen

Unwelcome Echoes 73

Chapter Fourteen

Countermoves 77

Chapter Fifteen

Smoke and Mirrors..85

Chapter Sixteen

The Leak...89

Chapter Seventeen

Fault Lines 93

Chapter Eighteen

Collateral..97

Chapter Nineteen

Unmasking...103

Chapter Twenty

Firebreak...107

Chapter Twenty-One

The Voice... 115

Chapter Twenty-Two

Breaking Point.. 121

Chapter Twenty-Three

Prebunk 125

Chapter Twenty-Four

Fault Lines in Daylight.......................................133

Chapter Twenty-Five

Splinter..137

Chapter Twenty-Six

The False Resurrection.. 141

Chapter Twenty-Seven

Fire in the Glass 145

Chapter Twenty-Eight

The Glass Trap 151

Chapter Twenty-Nine

Check and Countercheck 157

Chapter Thirty

Endgame..165

Epilogue

The Quiet Between Moves 169

About the Author..172

Prologue

Giselle always had a way with men. There was just something about her—an invisible pull—that made them fall hard and fast. But what most didn't realize until it was too late was that Giselle was toxic as hell.

Everywhere she went, she left broken hearts behind like souvenirs, without even trying. If you asked anyone close to her what her secret was, they'd just shrug. No one could figure her out.

Her own mother gave her away when she was just a little girl, convinced Giselle only wanted attention—and her boyfriends. The only person who ever showed her patience was Aunt Alicia.

Alicia was older than her mother and stricter too, but she never made Giselle feel judged. She gave her structure and a kind of love that was rare— unshakeable.

Growing up without a father and watching her mother switch men like outfits made Giselle suspicious of every man she met, even the ones in her own family. In her eyes, they were all the same—and they all deserved to be treated like they would leave eventually.

Even the good ones, the ones who tried to prove they were different, didn't stand a chance. Keeping her guard up 24/7 was exhausting, but Giselle didn't know any other way to be. And she wasn't open to changing.

Not yet anyway.

Chapter One

"Just Another Night"

Giselle never stayed in one place too long. Cities bored her. People wore out quickly. Routines? Those were for women who wanted rings, kids, and joint bank accounts—none of which Giselle had time for. Movement was survival, and survival meant never letting anyone pin her down.

Tonight, was like any other Thursday. The kind of night she pretended wasn't predictable even though she'd chosen the same lounge for the third week in a row. Vibe Lounge was tucked between two forgettable storefronts in the city's arts district. From the street, it looked like nothing—a dark window, a metal door with no sign. But inside, it felt like stepping into a secret. Dim lights pooled in corners, the hum of old-school R&B blended with the clink of glasses, and the air carried the faint smell of whiskey and ambition.

She slid onto a stool, red lips and high ponytail in place, thigh-high boots gleaming under the low lights. She looked like trouble. Because she was. That was the point. Trouble kept people guessing. Trouble kept people away.

Her drink came quick—tequila with lime. She swirled the glass lazily, watching the ice clink against itself. She wasn't waiting for anyone. She never waited.

"Can I buy you a drink?"

The voice came smooth, confident enough to think it would work. Giselle didn't even look up. Smooth was practice. Smooth meant this wasn't his first attempt tonight. She didn't deal with amateurs who thought charm was a shortcut.

"You can buy yourself one and keep it moving," she replied, cool as the glass in her hand.

A pause. Then laughter. "Damn. Alright then. Respect."

She smirked to herself as he walked away. Another one down. Another tiny reminder that she was untouchable if she wanted to be.

Her aunt Alicia's voice echoed faintly in her mind—*You're not going to meet anyone worth your time in a damn lounge, Giselle.* Maybe Alicia was right. But that was exactly the point. She wasn't looking for someone worth her time. She just needed someone who wouldn't waste too much of it.

Her phone buzzed on the counter. A text from Serena.

Serena: *You better not be out again. We have brunch in the morning.*

Giselle rolled her eyes but typed back, *Relax. One drink. Maybe two.* Which was mostly true. She left out the part about scanning the room for distraction like it was oxygen.

Across the lounge, her gaze landed on someone—different. A man sitting alone at the far end of the bar. No neon-colored cocktails, no overconfident grin. He didn't even glance at her. That unsettled her. Men looked. Always. That was the rule.

He tilted his glass—something dark, straight, no ice. His shoulders carried quiet strength, not the peacocking kind she was used to. His jaw was sharp, his eyes unreadable from this distance. The stillness about him annoyed her. It was like being ignored on purpose.

She didn't like being ignored.

Before she could talk herself out of it, she stood and crossed the room, heels clicking like a metronome against the floor. Every step was intentional, every movement meant to draw attention. If he noticed her coming, he didn't show it.

That alone made her want to slap the drink out of his hand just to see if he'd finally react.

"Is this seat taken?" she asked, pulling it out before he could answer.

He looked up at her then, and for the first time all night, Giselle felt something flicker in her chest. Not attraction exactly. Something sharper. Like recognition—but not from memory.

Older than she first guessed. Mid-thirties, maybe. His face was quiet, not the kind that begged to be liked. His eyes—deep brown, almost black—met hers directly. No hesitation. No smirk. Just direct.

"You're not the type to ask," he said evenly.

She arched a brow. "You don't know what type I am."

"No," he agreed. "Not yet."

Silence stretched between them. She waited for him to ask her name. He didn't. He went back to his drink, as if her presence changed nothing. Bold.

She turned toward him, lips curving. "So, what's your deal? Sit here ignoring beautiful women, sipping whiskey like some brooding noir character?"

That earned a flicker of a smile. Barely there. But it counted.

"You came over here, remember?" he said.

"Because you weren't looking at me," she countered.

"Maybe that was on purpose."

The soft laugh that escaped her surprised her. *And here I thought I was the difficult one.*

He finally gave her his name—*Malcolm.* And the way he said it, solid, like brick, made her file it away in her mind carefully.

She offered hers. *Giselle.*

"I figured," he said, eyes steady.

The audacity of that. And yet—she liked it.

Before she could push for more, his phone buzzed. He stood, dropped a hundred-dollar bill on the counter, and walked out. No number. No promise to call. Just gone.

Giselle sat frozen a moment, fingers curled tight around her glass. He'd left her with nothing—and somehow, that made her want him more.

$$Chapter\ Two$$

Mimosas & Mirrors

The sun was far too bright for how little sleep Giselle had gotten. She slipped into the booth at Palm & Pine, oversized sunglasses covering bloodshot eyes. The hangover wasn't from alcohol—she'd only had a few sips before Malcolm left—but from overthinking. The worst kind of hangover.

Palm & Pine was one of those brunch spots designed for Instagram. Fake greenery on the walls, pastel menus, overpriced lattes topped with edible glitter. The place smelled like syrup, perfume, and ambition. Couples leaned close across tables, families herded kids with iPads, and a group of college girls posed shamelessly for selfies over bottomless mimosas.

Serena was already there, sipping her mimosa through a straw like she had all the time in the world. She wore a fitted jumpsuit, nails sharp enough to count as weapons, and a face that said she'd slept soundly. She barely glanced up.

"You look like last night," Serena said, scrolling her phone with one hand.

Giselle tugged off her sunglasses, smirking despite herself. "And you look like a fashion ad for antidepressants."

"I receive that," Serena said, raising her glass in a lazy toast.

The server came by and Giselle ordered black coffee and bottomless mimosas—a contradiction that felt perfectly on brand. She slid into the booth across from her friend, resisting the urge to collapse sideways onto the cushion.

"So?" Serena finally looked up, eyes sharp. "What happened?"

"What makes you think something happened?"

"That text you sent? You only text like that when you're trying not to spiral."

"I literally said I was having one drink."

"You said *maybe two,* which in Giselle-math means you were either about to make out with a stranger… or commit a crime."

Giselle laughed, more than she meant to. "Okay, well, I didn't do either."

Serena leaned forward, a predator sniffing out blood. "But you met someone."

It wasn't a question.

Giselle pretended to be fascinated by the condensation on her water glass. "I didn't meet him. He was just… there."

"Uh-huh. And?"

"And he was weird."

Serena arched a brow. "Define weird."

"Like… emotionally fluent. Silent. Very *main character in an indie film who probably has trauma* energy."

"So basically, your type."

"No," Giselle shot back. "My type falls for me in ten minutes and ruins their own life trying to keep me. This one didn't even ask for my number."

Serena nearly spit out her mimosa. "Oof. You got curved?"

"I didn't get curved," Giselle said, stabbing the table with her manicured nail. "He just left."

"With a hundred-dollar tab and no phone number?"

"Exactly."

Serena grinned like a cat. "Sounds like a curve."

Giselle huffed, hiding her irritation behind her coffee cup. "It was the way he left. Like he knew I'd chase."

"And are you?"

"Hell no."

Long pause.

"…Probably not," Giselle admitted.

Their food arrived—avocado toast for Serena, chicken and waffles drowning in syrup for Giselle. Serena cut her toast with surgical precision while Giselle tore into her waffle like it owed her money.

"You know," Serena said between bites, "one day you're going to meet someone who doesn't play your game—and you're not going to know what to do with yourself."

"That sounds like a *them* problem."

Serena gave her a long look. "Giselle."

"What?"

"You act like men are puzzles. You break them down, solve them, toss them when they stop being interesting."

"Because they *do* stop being interesting."

"Maybe it's not them," Serena said quietly. "Maybe it's you. Maybe once they get close enough to see you—really see you—you pull the plug."

The words landed heavy. Giselle's jaw tightened, but she masked it with a smirk. "That's rich, coming from someone who broke up with a man because he used the wrong *there* in a text."

"That's called standards," Serena said smoothly, unbothered.

Giselle laughed, grateful for the lifeline back to humor. But Serena's words lingered, buzzing in the back of her skull.

She toyed with her fork, letting her mind drift. Aunt Alicia's voice surfaced, clear as if she were sitting at the table. *Baby, you can't keep pushing people away just to prove they were going to leave. Not everyone's your father. Not everyone's your mother.*

Giselle hated that memory. Hated that Aunt Alicia always knew the right nerve to press. She'd been seven, waiting by the window in her yellow dress for a father who never showed. And she'd been seventeen, being handed a duffel bag by her mother, told she was "too much to handle." The lesson stuck: people left. Always. And the trick to survival was leaving first.

"Earth to Giselle." Serena snapped her fingers. "Don't zone out while I'm lecturing."

"Sorry. I was just thinking about—" She stopped herself. *Nope. Not giving Serena that kind of ammo.*

"About Malcolm," Serena said, eyes gleaming.

Giselle froze. "I never told you his name."

"You didn't have to," Serena said smugly. "The way you're acting? Definitely a Malcolm. Nobody spirals over a Chad."

Giselle groaned. "You're insufferable."

"And yet, you love me." Serena raised her glass. "To men who don't play the game—and to us, who always win it anyway."

They clinked glasses, but Giselle's mind wasn't on the toast. She kept replaying Malcolm's calm eyes, the way he walked away like she was an afterthought. It should've bruised her ego, but instead it left her restless.

For the first time in years, she wondered what it would be like to lose the game and not hate it.

Chapter Three

Control Issues

By Monday, Giselle had almost convinced herself she didn't care.

Almost.

She buried herself in work, the way she always did when her brain wanted to gnaw on something she couldn't control. Distraction was her drug of choice. And work? Work was endless.

Her office was perched on the twelfth floor of a renovated warehouse, all exposed brick and trendy Edison bulbs. She ran a small digital branding firm—startups, fashion houses, influencers who wanted to look richer than they were. She made other people interesting for a living, and she was damn good at it.

The morning passed in a blur of emails and edits. A client wanted their logo "more minimalist but also more eye-catching." Another thought his personal brand needed "mystery" but also "approachability." Giselle rolled her eyes at both requests but delivered exactly what they wanted anyway. She always did. That was the game: take half-baked ideas, dress them up, and sell them back like gospel.

If she was honest, she liked the power of it—how people paid her to reinvent their identities while she never let anyone close enough to figure out hers. It was easier to sculpt someone else's story than to live in her own.

Her phone buzzed on the desk. Three unread texts from Jason. She'd gone on two dates with him, both forgettable. His face was already fading in her memory. She ignored the messages and went back to her screen.

But Malcolm kept interrupting her thoughts like static. His quiet voice replayed in her head. *You're not the type to ask. Maybe that was on purpose.* She hated how those words clung, how they pricked at the edges of her armor.

By noon, she slammed her laptop shut, too restless to sit still. She grabbed her bag and keys, telling herself she just needed coffee and fresh air. Anything to reset. Her heels clicked against the pavement as she moved through the city like she owned it. People stepped aside without her asking. She always walked that way—head high, sunglasses on, like nothing could touch her.

The line at Café Bloom was long. Too long. Freelancers with laptops, moms juggling strollers, couples whispering over shared pastries. Giselle hated couples. Not because she was bitter—she just didn't trust people who smiled that much before 2 p.m.

She ordered her default: iced vanilla oat milk latte. Then she moved to the side, phone in hand, pretending to scroll through emails. In reality, she was watching everyone else, reading them like case studies. The nervous guy rehearsing a pitch. The girl on her third "candid" selfie attempt. The couple with identical smiles. She catalogued them all, sharp and detached.

Then she heard it.

The voice.

Low. Calm. Unmistakable.

"Yeah, I'll take a black coffee. Room for cream."

Her pulse jumped. She turned before she could stop herself. And there he was. Malcolm. Two people away in line. Same dark jacket, same stillness, like he carried silence in his pocket.

He hadn't seen her yet.

For a second, she considered leaving. She could walk out right now, and he'd never know she'd been here. But the thought annoyed her. Giselle didn't run. Not from anyone.

So she cleared her throat, leaned against the counter, and said, "Didn't peg you for a cream-in-your-coffee type."

He looked up, recognition flickering across his face. Not shock, not even much surprise. Just that same cool acknowledgment.

"Didn't peg you for a morning person," he replied.

She smirked. "I'm not."

Malcolm took his coffee, stepped out of line, and waited near the door. She joined him, her latte in hand, the air between them thick with something unsaid.

"You live around here?" she asked, trying to sound casual.

"Yeah. A few blocks away."

"Of course you do," she muttered.

He tilted his head slightly. "You following me?"

The deadpan delivery pulled a laugh out of her before she could stop it. "You wish."

He sipped his coffee. "Twice in one week. That's either fate… or bad planning."

Her smirk faltered. The word *fate* sat wrong in her chest, too heavy, too hopeful. She brushed it off. "You always this hard to read?"

"Maybe." He studied her, gaze steady. "You always this interested?"

That stung. Not because it wasn't true, but because he said it like fact, not flirtation.

"Wow," she said, trying to recover. "You really don't care what people think of you, huh?"

"Not really," he said. "Should I?"

"No," she answered too quickly. Her defenses pricked.

They stood there, silence stretching between them. He didn't move closer. Didn't flirt. Just existed in his own calm, which somehow made her more restless. Most men tried to impress her, to win her over with attention or ego. Malcolm gave her nothing, and somehow that felt like too much.

Finally, he nodded once. "Nice seeing you again, Giselle."

And just like that, he walked off down the street. No number. No breadcrumb trail to follow.

She stood rooted to the sidewalk, latte sweating in her hand, watching him disappear into the crowd.

This was not how it was supposed to go. Men didn't walk away from her. Men didn't leave *her* with questions.

And somehow, that made her want him more.

She tossed her half-empty cup in the trash, the taste suddenly too sweet. As she walked back toward her office, her mind spun faster than her heels against the pavement. Maybe she was losing her edge. Maybe he was just a glitch in her system.

But deep down, in the quiet part of herself she hated to acknowledge, Giselle knew the truth. Malcolm wasn't a glitch. He was the kind of problem she couldn't solve with charm or control.

And for the first time in years, she wasn't sure if she wanted to.

Chapter Four

Unwanted Patterns

By midweek, Giselle was irritated with herself. She wasn't supposed to be thinking about him at all.

Men came and went, that was the rhythm she had mastered. Sometimes they left gifts, sometimes they left bruises—never anything worth keeping. But Malcolm had left her nothing, and somehow that absence was louder than any ring or apology or bouquet.

Wednesday night found her in her apartment, sprawled across the couch, glass of red wine balanced on her stomach. The city buzzed outside her window—sirens in the distance, the occasional honk of a horn, voices of late-night wanderers echoing up from the street. Her loft was sleek, curated like a mood board: abstract art, metallic accents, plants that survived on neglect. Everything in its place, nothing sentimental.

She told herself she was fine. Serena had dragged her through a spin class earlier and then tried to set her up with a banker she'd met at the juice bar. Giselle had rolled her eyes so hard she thought they'd get stuck. The banker smiled too much, asked too many questions. She declined his number. Serena said she was impossible. Giselle didn't argue.

Now, alone, she let the quiet settle in. Too much quiet always pulled at the threads she kept tucked away, but tonight she didn't fight it.

Her phone buzzed. A text from Troy. *Thinking of you.*

She stared at it, lips curling into a humorless smile. Of course he was. Troy only thought of her when his marriage hit turbulence. She typed back, *Don't,* and tossed her phone aside.

The glass in her hand trembled slightly as she remembered the last time she'd let Troy back in, months ago, against every warning she'd given herself. His cologne had clung to her pillows for days after, making her feel sick and weak. Aunt Alicia had called the situation what it was: *you're addicted to men who can't give you anything real, baby.*

Maybe she was addicted to the ache. Maybe she was addicted to proving Alicia wrong.

The knock at her door startled her. She wasn't expecting anyone.

She padded across the hardwood in bare feet, glass still in hand. Through the peephole she saw Serena's familiar outline, tapping her nails impatiently on her phone.

"Open up before I chip a nail," Serena's muffled voice came.

Giselle swung the door open. "You ever think about calling first?"

"No," Serena said, breezing in like she owned the place. She carried takeout bags that smelled like Thai curry and fried rice. "Dinner. You owe me for suffering through spin class with you."

"I recall you screaming at the instructor to play Beyoncé," Giselle said, shutting the door.

"Exactly. That class would've killed me if not for Queen Bey."

They settled on the couch with cartons spread across the coffee table. Serena cracked open a spring roll, eyeing Giselle. "So… banker boy?"

"No," Giselle said flatly.

"Why not? He was cute, rich, gainfully employed. What's the problem?"

"Too available."

Serena groaned. "God forbid a man actually wants you."

Giselle stabbed at her noodles with chopsticks. "Wanting me isn't the problem. Thinking they deserve to keep me is."

Serena shook her head. "Girl, you are allergic to stability."

"Stability is just another word for boring."

"Or safe," Serena countered.

They ate in silence for a while, the only sounds the rustle of containers and the hum of traffic outside.

Finally, Serena set her food down. "This is about him, isn't it? The lounge guy. Malcolm."

Giselle's hand tightened around her chopsticks. "It's not about him."

"You've mentioned him, like, three times without realizing it."

"I have not."

"You have." Serena leaned in, grin sharp. "So, what is it? He fine?"

"He's... different." The words slipped out before Giselle could swallow them back.

"Different how?"

"He didn't want anything from me."

Serena blinked. "And that's bad?"

"It's unusual," Giselle corrected.

Serena let out a low whistle. "Oh, girl. You're spiraling. He ignored you, and now you're obsessed."

Giselle glared. "I'm not obsessed."

"You're drinking wine alone in the dark, replaying his every word."

"That's called reflection."

"That's called denial."

They stared at each other until both burst out laughing, tension cracking just enough to breathe.

But later, after Serena left and the apartment was silent again, Giselle admitted what she hadn't dared to say aloud: Malcolm unsettled her because he hadn't played the game. He hadn't tried to win her. He hadn't tried to save her. He'd just seen her—and walked away.

She poured herself another glass of wine, ignoring the voice in her head whispering Aunt Alicia's words: *You can't control everything, Giselle. And you can't keep running every time someone gets close.*

The problem was, control was all she had. Without it, she was that little girl in the yellow dress again, waiting for a father who never showed.

She closed her eyes and told herself she wasn't waiting now. She was choosing. Always choosing.

Still, when she finally drifted to sleep, her dreams betrayed her. She saw Malcolm's steady gaze, unbothered, unbroken—and woke with her pulse racing, as if she had lost something she never even had.

Chapter Five

Background Check

It started with a knock that sounded like it knew her schedule—three clipped taps, confident, unapologetic. Giselle didn't need to check the peephole to guess. Only one person knocked like she paid rent there.

She opened the door to Serena, who swept in with the weather and the smell of street rain, clutching an iced coffee in one hand and a tote fat with paper in the other. Her braids were piled into a crown, nails razor-sharp, expression brighter than should be legal on a weekday afternoon.

"What did you do?" Giselle asked, already moving aside.

Serena gave a mock gasp. "Hello to you too. I brought gifts."

"You brought evidence," Giselle said, eyeing the tote as the door clicked shut. "What did you find?"

Serena tossed the tote onto the dining table like a mic drop. "A better question," she said, fishing out a manila folder, "is what didn't I find?"

Giselle crossed her arms, a reflex she mistook for patience. "Serena."

"Relax. I did not hack the Pentagon." She popped the straw between lip gloss and took a slow pull. "I used the free internet like a responsible citizen."

"You used the paid internet," Giselle said, because she knew her. "You paid someone."

Serena didn't deny it. She fanned the folder open, sliding out printouts: property records, corporate filings, screen captures with highlighted lines, a blurry newspaper photo clipped from some financial blog. Paper whispered against wood; the apartment felt suddenly like a small newsroom lit by expensive lamps.

"Start here," Serena said, tapping the first page. "County deed. Breckridge Avenue. Brownstone, three stories, garden level. Buyer: Malcolm T. Harrington. Purchase date: six months ago."

Giselle skimmed the page, lips tightening. "Mortgage?"

"None." Serena's smile was part triumph, part alarm. "Paid cash. Title is clean. No liens. Closed in twenty-one days."

"Cash?" Giselle repeated, trying to make the word feel less heavy. In her line of work, cash meant power or caution—sometimes both. "People with nothing to hide don't usually throw around that kind of quiet."

Serena flipped to the next page. "Then there's this." A screenshot from a news article with a headline that tried too hard to sound neutral: **Family Tragedy Delays Trial in Investment Fraud Case.** The photo underneath showed a younger Malcolm in a dark suit, expression grave beside a woman with perfect lipstick and eyes that didn't match the smile.

Giselle felt the air thin. "Read it."

Serena skimmed aloud. "—Harrington Investment Group… elder son Elias Harrington… alleged embezzlement… offshore accounts… whistleblower identified as younger brother, Malcolm… family dispute… disappearance of Elias complicates prosecution." She paused, glancing up. "There's more, but you get the gist."

"He blew the whistle," Giselle said, more to herself than to Serena. It made sense and didn't. She pictured that steady gaze, the quiet, the weight he carried like it fit his shoulders. "And then he vanished."

"Left his firm," Serena confirmed. "Sold off a bunch of positions. Went dark for almost a year. Resurfaces here, buys a house in cash, keeps his head down. If he's trying to be boring, he's almost succeeding."

"Almost," Giselle murmured, flipping another page. The paper burned cold under her thumb. She hated how quickly her brain started building a picture: motives, timelines, the angles where truth might hide. It was the same skill she used in branding—assemble the shards, tell a story the eye believes.

Serena leaned a hip against the table. "You want the human version or the spreadsheet version?"

"The truth," Giselle said. "Whichever one that is."

"Spreadsheet first," Serena said, because she was Serena. "He moved money right before the house purchase. Nothing illegal on the surface, but very… careful. Tax records show a sharp dip in earned income last year, then a lump from asset liquidation. If anyone asked me to guess, I'd say he burned his old life to the ground and brought only what he could carry."

"And the human version?"

Serena's voice softened. "He's the brother who stayed to clean it up. Or the brother who couldn't live with staying. Depending on who's telling it."

Silence unspooled between them, thin and delicate. Outside, traffic stitched the late afternoon together; somewhere a car alarm yawned and gave up. Giselle stared at the photo again. Younger Malcolm. Same set to the mouth. Same eyes that didn't beg.

"I know that look," she said quietly.

"What look?"

"A person who doesn't expect anyone to believe him." She set the page down. "Or to stay."

Serena watched her for a beat, then exhaled. "I was going to save this part for dessert, but you look like you need the whole cake." She pulled another printout: a local blog post with too many ads. At the bottom, a single paragraph about a hospital fundraiser. The caption beneath a photo of donors: *Attendees included Malcolm Harrington and Eva Sloane.*

"Eva?" Giselle asked, pulse hitching at the name without knowing why.

"Journalist," Serena said. "Used to cover the business beat. Wrote about the Harrington case, then disappeared from bylines for a while. She shows up again—once—with him at a fundraiser, and then… nothing."

"Girlfriend?"

"Friend." Serena tilted her head. "Or witness. Or problem. Hard to say."

Giselle hated speculation dressed as answers, even her own. She slid the page back. "How long did you spend on this?"

"Enough," Serena said, unbothered. "Don't scold me for protecting my friend."

"I'm not scolding." Giselle rubbed at a spot on the table that didn't exist. "I'm… trying to decide if I should be grateful or furious."

"Try both." Serena's voice softened again. "Look, I know how you are with ghosts in expensive suits. I just wanted to make sure this one doesn't become a habit you can't quit."

The line landed with too much accuracy. Giselle thought of Troy's text—*Thinking of you*—and the way her fingers had itched to open the door to an old ache. She thought of Malcolm's quiet, the unshowy way he occupied space. The ache wasn't the same. That was the problem.

Serena folded her arms. "Tell me what you're thinking. The real version."

Giselle tried to smirk and couldn't find the muscles for it. "I'm thinking I hate men who arrive with footnotes."

"And?"

"And," she admitted, "I'm thinking I recognized him before I knew his name."

Serena blinked. "Meaning?"

"Meaning he felt like a room I've stood in before," Giselle said. "Not the furniture, not the paint. The temperature." She shook her head, annoyed with herself for the poetry of it. "Forget it."

"No, keep going," Serena said, lips quirking. "I like when you get metaphysical. It makes you sloppy."

Giselle lifted the photo again, holding it at arm's length. The woman beside Malcolm—the perfect lipstick—looked like one of those people who turn secrets into currency. A journalist, Serena had said. If Malcolm had let a journalist stand beside him in public, he either trusted her completely or needed her more than he wanted to admit.

Aunt Alicia's voice rose like steam from a kettle: *Baby, you keep acting like knowing everything will save you from anything. It won't.*

Giselle set the photo down. "What do you expect me to do with this?"

"Whatever you want," Serena said. "You asked me to never let you walk blind. I'm not letting you."

"I didn't ask," Giselle said, but the protest was soft, habit not conviction.

Serena reached across the table and tapped the property record with a nail. "Start with neutral facts. He owns a house. He paid cash. He keeps to himself. He's connected to a family mess but not in the way you think. If you see him again, you'll have better questions."

"If?" Giselle echoed before she could stop herself.

Serena grinned. "There it is."

Giselle rolled her eyes because it was easier than rolling back time. She gathered the papers into a more orderly pile, as if tidiness could make meaning. Her reflection in the window caught her: expensive hair, steady mouth, eyes that did not forgive. She didn't recognize the softness Serena always claimed was there. Maybe Serena wanted to believe in something she couldn't see.

"Do you want me to send you the links?" Serena asked, already pulling out her phone.

"No." Giselle surprised herself with the speed of the answer. "I don't want to fall into a hole I can't climb out of."

"Too late," Serena said lightly. "But noted."

They let the quiet return. Serena sipped her coffee; Giselle traced the corner of the photo until the paper flared warm under her fingertip. She tried to imagine walking into that brownstone, the smell of its hallways, the feel of its banister under her palm. She pictured Malcolm's kitchen, tidy and underfurnished, the kind of order a person chooses when chaos has already cost them too much.

"Do you think he's dangerous?" Giselle asked finally.

Serena didn't answer right away. "I think he's inconvenient," she said. "Which is sometimes the same thing."

Giselle breathed out slowly. She could live with inconvenient. She had built an entire life on refusing to rearrange for anyone else. But danger—danger forced you to tell the truth about what you were willing to lose.

She slid the papers back into the folder and closed it. The sound felt like a hinge seating in place.

Serena reached for the folder, then thought better and left it where it lay. "You okay?"

"I don't know," Giselle said, which was the most honest thing she'd said all week.

Serena's mouth curved—not into a smile, exactly, but something kinder. "That's a start."

They moved to the couch without planning to. Serena stretched out and flicked through channels like she could erase tension with static. Giselle sat upright, the folder within reach, as if the paper might answer questions if she stared hard enough.

On the screen, a game show audience clapped on command. Someone shrieked over a blender. Serena snorted. "Capitalism is exhausting."

"Everything is," Giselle said, eyes still on the papers. "Especially people."

"Especially you," Serena teased, leaning her head on the arm of the couch. "Promise me one thing."

"No promises," Giselle said automatically.

"Then a suggestion. If you see him again, don't pretend you don't want to. Take the meeting. Ask the questions. You can always walk away later."

"Walking away is my religion," Giselle said.

Serena's look softened. "Maybe try a sabbatical."

They let the TV fill the room. The rain outside eased to a whisper; the city exhaled. When Serena finally stood to leave, she squeezed Giselle's shoulder, a quick press that said: alive, here, not leaving.

When the door closed, the apartment felt bigger and too quiet. Giselle stood at the table for a long moment, then slid the folder into a drawer she kept for things that mattered and shouldn't. She told herself she wouldn't open it again. She told herself a lot of things she didn't believe.

In bed, sleep refused to behave. When it finally arrived, it brought dreams she could not catalog: a brownstone staircase, a woman with red lipstick and cold eyes, a door that would not open no matter how gently she turned the handle. She woke before dawn with a hand pressed to her chest, like she'd been holding something there in the dark.

The feeling didn't fade. Not with coffee. Not with the shower running too hot. She dressed in black and steel and the right amount of perfume, and when she passed the drawer on her way out, she did not pause.

On the street, the city had that washed-clean smell it gets after a night of rain. Her heels found the rhythm of the sidewalk. People moved around her, busy with their own scripts. Giselle lifted her chin and joined the flow, telling herself the same thing she always told herself when the ground started to tilt: it's fine, it's nothing, you're in control.

And then, as if summoned by a thought she refused to name, she turned the corner onto Breckridge without thinking why—and looked up at a brownstone whose brick seemed to know her secrets.

Chapter Six

The Brownstone

The brownstone was older than its clean facade suggested, a quiet monument standing between two newer renovations that shouted for attention with their glass balconies and neon-trimmed foyers. Malcolm's building didn't shout. It kept its history folded inward, the kind of house that looked ordinary until you realized it had survived fires, markets, and wars without being rebuilt.

Giselle hated how quickly she noticed that about it. She was supposed to be walking without purpose, heels tapping the sidewalk in rhythm with the midmorning flow of commuters. Supposed to be detached. But her body slowed when the brickwork came into view, like her pulse had its own memory of the place.

She stopped across the street, pretending to check her phone. No notifications. She typed a message to herself just to look occupied: *stop it.*

The blinds in the second-floor window were tilted open, but the interior was unreadable. No movement. The front steps were swept clean. The wrought-iron railing gleamed as if polished that morning. She tried to picture him there, unlocking the door, carrying groceries, moving through a life he clearly didn't want anyone to trace.

Her chest tightened. This was stupid. Serena would laugh herself into a coma if she saw her now, loitering like a bad private detective. Giselle had built an entire brand on never chasing. And yet here she was, circling a house like a moth that couldn't resist the flame.

The street shifted around her. A delivery truck pulled up, blocking her view. She stepped closer to the curb, annoyed at herself for caring, more annoyed at herself for waiting. The driver jumped out, slamming the door, carting boxes toward a doorway two houses down.

When the truck rolled forward again, the brownstone's door was open.

Malcolm stood on the stoop, keys in hand, dressed in a charcoal jacket and jeans. Nothing flashy, but he wore the clothes like they had been made for him. His posture was as steady as she remembered, the weight of his silence radiating outward.

He saw her.

There was no hesitation. His eyes met hers across the street, and the world tilted. For a heartbeat, it felt less like recognition and more like inevitability.

Giselle raised her chin, masking the sudden rush under a practiced smirk. "So this is where you hide," she called, voice carrying lightly over the traffic.

Malcolm locked the door behind him before answering. "And this is where you loiter?"

Her laugh came sharp, cutting tension she couldn't admit was hers. "Coincidence."

"Of course." His tone was unreadable, a flat line that could cut either way.

She crossed the street without waiting for an invitation. Her heels clicked against asphalt, her shadow stretching long in the slant of the morning sun. Up close, the air around him felt the same as before: grounded, unshaken, like standing near a tree that had seen too many storms to be impressed by the next one.

"You're full of surprises, Malcolm Harrington," she said. She wanted the name to taste like a dare.

He didn't flinch. "You've done your homework."

She arched a brow. "Homework implies effort. I don't chase."

"And yet you're here."

The simple observation made her stomach tighten. She hated being caught in contradictions. "I was in the neighborhood."

"Coincidence," he echoed, as if trying the word on his tongue.

They stood in silence for a beat, the city moving around them. A woman with a stroller glanced up at them, then away quickly, as if sensing something private and tense.

"Are you going to invite me in?" Giselle asked finally.

Malcolm's gaze held hers. Not hostile, not warm—just steady. "Do you want me to?"

The question landed heavier than it should. Because yes, she did. And no, she didn't. Both truths stretched taut in her chest.

Instead of answering, she shrugged. "Depends on what kind of secrets you're hiding in there."

His mouth curved slightly—half amusement, half warning. "Secrets are rarely kind to their visitors."

That should have been the end of it. He should have walked away, left her smirking on the sidewalk, preserved his mystery. But instead, he unlocked the door again and pushed it open.

"Five minutes," he said.

Inside, the air was cool and faintly citrus, like someone who cleaned often but without obsession. The living room was spare: leather sofa, iron floor lamp, shelves with more emptiness than books. No family photos. No clutter. It wasn't the home of a man settled; it was the shelter of someone passing through.

She trailed a finger along the edge of the shelf. "Minimalist chic, or hiding the evidence?"

"Neither," Malcolm said, setting his keys in a bowl by the door. "Just easier to live with less."

"You sound like a monk."

He glanced at her, expression unreadable. "You sound disappointed."

Giselle smiled tightly, masking the prickle under her skin. "I expected… more."

"More what?"

She wanted to say more warmth, more life, more signs of the man behind the stare. Instead, she let her eyes drift across the room. "More proof you're not a ghost."

His silence stretched, filling the space like a held breath.

Finally, he said, "You don't really want proof. You want a puzzle."

"And you don't?" she shot back.

His gaze met hers, steady, unwavering. "I'm tired of puzzles."

The words landed like a stone, solid and heavy. Giselle folded her arms, hiding the way they shook slightly. She hated when people said things that stuck too easily.

The sound of footsteps broke the silence. She stiffened, glancing toward the staircase. Malcolm followed her gaze calmly.

"Upstairs neighbor," he said. "She's eighty-seven. Wears slippers shaped like cats."

Relief came sharp and quick, followed by irritation at herself for needing it. "Convenient alibi," she muttered.

His brow lifted. "You think I brought you here to hurt you?"

"I think people are rarely what they pretend to be," she said.

For the first time, something flickered across his face—something like pain, gone too quickly to name.

"You're right," he said quietly. "But neither are you."

The words cut deeper than she wanted to admit. She turned toward the door, armor snapping back into place. "My five minutes are up."

"Your choice," Malcolm said, unbothered.

On the street again, sunlight felt harsher. She walked fast, trying to shake the sensation of his gaze following her. But it wasn't his stare she couldn't escape—it was his words. *Neither are you.*

She hated how much she wanted to know what he thought that meant.

And across the street, in the reflection of a shop window, she caught the faintest outline of a man leaning against a parked car. Not Malcolm. Someone else. Watching.

When she turned fully, the space was empty. Just a car, door shut, windows blank.

Still, the pulse in her throat hammered as she walked away.

Chapter Seven

The Watchers

Giselle didn't go home right away.

Her heels carried her through blocks of storefronts and bus stops, past vendors setting up fruit carts, past mothers tugging at distracted children. She blended into the crowd as she always did—expensive hair, sharp sunglasses, body language that declared she wasn't to be bothered. But inside, her pulse was a staccato beat she couldn't slow.

The reflection in the shop window replayed in her mind. A man. Or a shadow that wanted to look like one. Watching. She'd turned, and he'd vanished. Ghost or flesh, she couldn't shake the certainty that he had been there.

She ducked into a bookstore, letting the cool hush of the air-conditioning calm her nerves. The place smelled of paper and dust, safety wrapped in spines. She didn't even care what section she wandered into; the point was distance. She trailed her fingers along a shelf of mysteries, smirking at the irony. The titles promised answers in three hundred pages. Her life rarely granted them at all.

She pulled down a random book, flipped it open. Words blurred. All she saw was the brownstone's clean brick, the way Malcolm's voice had carved into her: *You're not what you pretend to be.* The echo clung, merging with Aunt Alicia's old refrain: *Baby, the masks you wear don't protect you. They strangle you.*

She shoved the book back onto the shelf harder than she meant to. A man at the end of the aisle glanced up. Not Malcolm. Not the shadow.

Just a stranger with tired eyes. Still, she moved away quickly, telling herself she wasn't running.

By the time she reached her apartment, dusk was falling. The sky glowed bruised purple, city lights bleeding through. She closed the door and slid the locks into place with more force than usual. The loft was neat, ordered, waiting. But tonight, it didn't feel like hers. The corners seemed deeper, the windows thinner.

She poured a glass of wine and carried it to the window, scanning the street below. Normal traffic. A delivery van. A couple arguing by the crosswalk. Nothing out of place.

Still, her shoulders stayed tense.

The buzz of her phone on the counter jolted her. She snatched it up, expecting Troy again, or Serena. Instead, it was an unknown number.

Did you enjoy your visit?

The glass nearly slipped from her hand.

She reread the words twice, three times, as if they might rearrange into something harmless. They didn't. No name. No context. Just that.

Her first thought was Malcolm. But that wasn't his style. He didn't strike her as a man who played games with texts. If he wanted to ask a question, he'd do it to her face.

The second thought made her throat go dry: the watcher. Whoever had stood outside that brownstone. Whoever might still be standing somewhere now.

She typed back before she could stop herself: *Who is this?*

The reply came faster than she liked. *Someone who knows you see more than you should.*

Her heart slammed once, twice, too hard. She set the phone down on the counter like it had burned her fingers.

For several minutes, she just stood there, staring at the screen, waiting for another message. None came.

The silence grew teeth.

She carried the phone into the bedroom, set it on the nightstand, and paced. Her reflection in the mirror looked too composed, as if her face had learned long ago how to lie. But her hands betrayed her, trembling slightly no matter how tightly she curled them into fists.

It wasn't fear exactly. It was recognition. She knew this feeling, though she hated admitting it. Growing up with a mother who treated men like rotating passwords, who changed the locks every six months, Giselle had learned early how to sense when something was about to shift. Danger wasn't always loud. Sometimes it was just the quiet reminder that you were already seen.

The phone buzzed again. A photo this time.

Her, outside the bookstore an hour ago, hand on a shelf, eyes cast down.

The caption: *Nice choice. You always did like mysteries.*

Her knees almost gave. She sat hard on the bed, glass spilling red onto the white comforter. She didn't care.

She tried to think. Serena. She should call Serena. But what would she say? That someone was trailing her with a camera, that her face was a headline waiting to happen? Serena would tell her to get out, stay out, run. Running wasn't Giselle's style.

Instead, she stared at the photo again. Whoever sent it wasn't sloppy. They'd been close enough to capture her clearly, far enough she hadn't noticed. That took practice.

She deleted the text, then the number. Futile, she knew. But it gave her the illusion of control.

That night, she dreamed of doors again. Endless doors, lined up in corridors that stretched like veins. Some opened to empty rooms.

Some to fire. One opened to Malcolm's face, half-shadowed, telling her nothing she didn't already know: *You're not what you pretend to be.*

She woke with sweat cooling on her skin and the city morning spilling gold across her floor.

By nine a.m., she had armor back in place: silk blouse, pencil skirt, hair sleek, lips sharp red. The world would see the woman who controlled every room she entered. Only she would know the panic pacing beneath.

At her desk, she tried to drown in client emails. A cosmetics startup wanted a "rebrand that feels both radical and timeless." A real estate developer demanded "luxury that feels approachable." She answered them all in cool, practiced lines. But every click of the keyboard felt like a lie.

Her office window faced the street. Across it, on the sidewalk, a man leaned against a lamppost, face obscured by a cap. He wasn't moving. He wasn't scrolling a phone like everyone else.

He was just waiting.

Giselle stared for too long before jerking the blinds shut.

The rest of the day dragged. By evening, Serena was calling, her voice all casual brightness. "Drinks tonight. No excuses."

Giselle almost said no. Almost confessed. But her pride was louder. "Fine. Eight."

She hung up, stared at the folder she'd shoved into her drawer days ago, and wondered if the problem wasn't Malcolm after all. Maybe the problem was that someone else already knew how much she wanted to understand him.

And maybe—terrifyingly—they understood her better than she dared admit.

Chapter Eight

Unsettled Ground

The bar Serena chose was the opposite of subtle. Neon lights pulsed behind the counter, bottles gleaming like gemstones on display. Music throbbed low but insistent, the kind that kept people moving without realizing they were swaying. Clusters of after-work crowds filled the booths, laughter mixing with the sharp clink of ice against glass.

Giselle stepped inside like she owned the place, every inch of her styled to command attention: black silk blouse, gold hoops, the kind of lipstick that looked like it dared you to smudge it. No one would guess her stomach had been in knots since morning, or that she'd nearly thrown her phone into traffic after the second anonymous text.

Serena waved from a corner booth, two glasses already waiting. She looked like casual perfection—denim jacket over a slip dress, sneakers gleaming white, braids coiled into a bun. When Serena leaned back, the whole room seemed to orbit her.

"You're late," Serena said as Giselle slid into the booth.

"I'm dramatic," Giselle countered, forcing a smile. She reached for the drink without asking what it was. Vodka, lime, a bite of something herbal. Strong enough.

Serena studied her over the rim of her glass. "You look… tense."

"I'm fine."

"You say that like someone who's about to set a building on fire."

"That's oddly specific."

"Because I've seen it. Not literally, but close." Serena leaned in, lowering her voice. "What happened?"

Giselle toyed with the straw, swirling ice she didn't care to drink. She wanted to say nothing, but Serena's gaze had always been too sharp, too steady. "Work's annoying. Men are worse. Same as always."

Serena arched a brow. "So Malcolm again."

"Why do you keep bringing him up?"

"Because you keep dodging every other subject."

Giselle smirked, though it felt brittle. "You're exhausting."

"And you're lying," Serena shot back, but her tone softened. "Seriously, G. What's going on? You've been twitchy since brunch, and that's saying something."

For a moment, Giselle considered telling her everything—the texts, the photo, the man at the lamppost. The words lined up behind her teeth like prisoners waiting for release. But pride clamped down. Pride always did.

Instead, she shrugged. "I saw him again. Outside his place."

Serena set her drink down slowly. "You went to his house?"

"I was in the neighborhood."

"Coincidence," Serena echoed, disbelief clear.

"Exactly," Giselle said, as if saying it twice made it true.

Serena sighed. "You know, normal people don't stalk men they barely know."

"Stalk is such an ugly word."

"What word would you like? Loiter? Hover? Obsess?"

"Observe," Giselle corrected smoothly. "I'm observing."

Serena laughed, sharp and incredulous. "Girl, you're spiraling."

"Maybe." Giselle leaned back, mask slipping into place again. "But at least I spiral in heels."

Their banter earned a smile from Serena, but her eyes still searched Giselle's face, looking for cracks.

Halfway through her second drink, Giselle felt the itch again—the certainty of being watched. Her gaze drifted over the bar, scanning faces. A man in a dark jacket sat two tables over, nursing a whiskey and pretending to scroll his phone. Nothing unusual. Except he hadn't looked down once since she walked in.

Her pulse ticked faster. She turned back quickly, plastering a smile for Serena's benefit.

"You're not listening to me," Serena accused.

"Sorry. What?"

"I said, maybe this Malcolm thing isn't about him at all. Maybe it's about you not knowing what to do when someone doesn't play your game."

"Or maybe it's about you needing better hobbies," Giselle deflected.

But the words rang hollow, even to her.

Serena leaned closer, voice dropping low. "Listen. Whoever he is, whatever you think you're doing—you better make sure you're the one in control. Because if you're not, Giselle…" She trailed off, shaking her head. "You don't handle losing well."

Giselle's smile sharpened. "I don't lose."

"Everyone loses eventually," Serena said softly.

The music shifted, bassline rolling deeper. For a second, it swallowed the space between them. Giselle finished her drink in a long swallow, not caring about the burn.

"Enough doom and gloom," she said, forcing brightness. "Tell me about you. Anyone new?"

Serena groaned, letting herself be steered. "I've been entertaining a chef who thinks his risotto is a love language. It's not."

Giselle laughed, relief disguised as mockery. "You and your tragic men."

"Pot, meet kettle," Serena muttered.

The conversation turned lighter, but Giselle's attention drifted. Every few minutes, her eyes flicked back to the man in the jacket. He was still there. Still scrolling nothing. Still too still.

By the time Serena dragged her onto the dance floor, Giselle's nerves buzzed. The press of bodies, the lights, the beat—it should have drowned the feeling out. Instead, it sharpened it. She felt eyes on her even in the crush of strangers.

She danced anyway, swaying with Serena, letting the rhythm disguise her unease. That was the trick—keep moving, keep shining, and no one noticed the cracks.

But when she finally returned to the booth, breathless and flushed, the man was gone. His drink sat unfinished.

A chill prickled her spine.

Serena flopped down beside her, laughing. "You're impossible to keep up with."

"Story of my life," Giselle murmured, scanning the bar again.

"Don't disappear on me," Serena warned, nudging her shoulder. "Not for some man, not for some mystery. Promise?"

Giselle didn't answer.

Because she couldn't promise something she wasn't sure she could keep.

Later, when she stepped out into the night air, the city felt too quiet for once. Serena had taken a car home, leaving Giselle to walk the few blocks back to her building. Neon buzzed overhead, footsteps echoed from alleys.

Halfway down the block, her phone buzzed.

Another text. No number.

Nice dress.

Her breath caught. She scanned the street. Empty. But the message felt like a hand pressing between her shoulder blades.

She quickened her pace, heels sharp against concrete.

By the time she reached her building and locked the door behind her, her mask had slipped entirely. She pressed her back to the door, chest heaving, and admitted what she'd denied all week.

This wasn't about Malcolm anymore.

Someone was watching her. And whoever they were, they weren't planning to stop.

Chapter Nine

Cracks in the Glass

Giselle told herself the text didn't matter.

She told herself in the mirror the next morning, lips painted the color of defiance, hair pinned sleek, blouse sharp enough to wound. She told herself again in the elevator ride up to her office, where the mirrored walls reflected her back fourfold, a chorus of Giselles all in control.

But when she unlocked her office door, the lie cracked.

On her desk sat a single white envelope. No markings. No postage. Just her name, printed in neat block letters.

Her pulse stuttered. She glanced toward the hall, but the floor was quiet, the usual shuffle of early arrivals muffled behind closed doors.

She slid the envelope open with deliberate calm, nails steady even as her stomach twisted.

Inside was a single photograph.

Her, last night, stepping into her apartment building. Head turned slightly, expression unreadable. The photo was crisp, taken from across the street.

Beneath it, a note in the same block letters: *You can't lock out what's already inside.*

She crumpled the paper in her fist, throat tight. Then, slowly, she smoothed it flat again. Control. Always control. If someone wanted her rattled, she wouldn't give them the satisfaction.

By the time her assistant poked her head in, Giselle had the photo tucked into a drawer, smile in place.

"Morning," the assistant chirped. "I moved the Baxter call to three."

"Perfect," Giselle said smoothly.

The girl lingered a moment, brow creasing. "You okay? You look…"

"Fine," Giselle cut in. Too sharp. The assistant nodded quickly and left.

Alone again, Giselle exhaled. Her reflection in the dark screen of her monitor looked like a stranger.

She buried herself in work. Logo revisions, email drafts, brand decks. But concentration fractured. Every time footsteps passed outside her door; her shoulders tightened. Every time her phone buzzed with a client notification; her pulse jumped.

At noon, Serena called.

"You sound like you're being haunted," Serena said after Giselle's clipped hello.

"Just working."

"You always say that when you're avoiding telling me something."

Giselle pinched the bridge of her nose. "You're exhausting."

"And you're unraveling," Serena shot back. "I can hear it. What's going on?"

"Nothing."

"Liar."

"Drop it."

Silence stretched. Then Serena's voice softened. "Giselle. If you don't tell me, I can't help you."

Help. The word snagged. Giselle almost laughed. What help could Serena offer against ghosts with cameras and keys to her quiet?

Still, she almost broke. Almost confessed about the texts, the photos, the watcher. But pride was stronger. Pride and fear—two poisons she knew too well.

"Everything's under control," she said instead.

"You don't sound like it," Serena murmured. "And when you finally admit it's not, I hope it's not too late."

The call ended with that heavy silence Giselle hated most—the kind that left her alone with herself.

She pushed through the rest of the day, robotic, efficient. By five, she was exhausted in ways coffee couldn't fix. She left the office with her chin high, scanning the street the way she always did now.

The city was alive: taxis honking, pedestrians weaving, lights blinking awake as dusk settled. Normal. Comforting in its chaos.

Until she noticed him.

Across the street, leaning against a lamppost—different from yesterday, but the same pose, the same stillness. Cap pulled low, jacket nondescript. Too ordinary to be ordinary.

Her steps slowed. His head tilted slightly, as if acknowledging her.

Something cold slid down her spine.

She turned sharply, heading the opposite direction, heels striking like punctuation. She didn't run. Giselle never ran. But her pulse did.

Three blocks later, she ducked into a crowded café. The line was long, voices loud, steam rising from espresso machines. Perfect cover. She ordered a coffee she didn't want and took a seat near the back, where she could watch the door.

Minutes passed. Customers came and went. No sign of the man.

She tried to breathe. Tried to tell herself she was imagining it. That the photo, the texts, the watcher—they were pieces of a puzzle her paranoia was assembling wrong.

Her phone buzzed.

She froze.

A new text. *Nice cover. The café suits you.*

Her vision blurred for half a second. She forced her hand steady, swiped the message away, and deleted it.

No one around her looked suspicious. A girl in a hoodie typing on a laptop. A couple whispering over a shared cupcake. An older man scrolling his phone. Normal. All normal.

But she knew better. Someone was here. Someone had their eyes on her right now.

She left the coffee untouched, gathered her bag, and slipped out through the side door.

By the time she reached her building again, night had fallen hard. The lobby light flickered once as she stepped inside. The doorman gave her a nod, oblivious.

In the elevator, she finally let her mask crack. Her reflection in the mirrored walls looked pale, eyes too wide, mouth too tight. She hated the fear she saw there.

When the doors opened on her floor, she forced herself back into control. She unlocked her door, slid the locks, checked the windows twice. Then she poured herself a drink and sat on the couch, phone in hand, waiting.

Waiting for the next text. The next photo. The next move in a game she hadn't agreed to play.

Hours passed. Midnight bled into two a.m. No messages came.

The silence was worse.

At last, she drifted into uneasy sleep on the couch.

And in the shadows across the street, unseen, a camera lens glinted once before disappearing into the dark.

57

Chapter Ten

Terms of Engagement

Morning arrived like a dare. The city wore a hard blue sky, the kind that made everything look sharper, crueler. Giselle dressed for war—charcoal blazer, crisp white shirt, hair pinned close to her skull, lipstick engineered not to budge. She studied herself in the mirror and practiced the face she wore for clients, for rivals, for anyone who thought they could read her: unbothered, uninterested, undefeated.

The envelope from yesterday sat in the drawer, a siren muted by wood. She did not open it again. She did not need to. The photo was burned into her mind—her body mid-step, caught between outside and in, the caption promising that locks were a courtesy, not a boundary.

Control is a choreography, she reminded herself. You decide where the light hits, you choose what stays in shadow.

By nine, she had a plan. Not a perfect one, but plans were never perfect; they were a statement of intent. She texted Serena—*Busy today. Don't worry about me.* A lie constructed for love. Then she searched her brain for the only person who could shift this feeling from the abstract to the accountable.

Malcolm.

The thought tasted like surrender and steel. He might be the center of the storm or a man caught in its weather; either way, proximity to him drew attention. If she confronted him, she risked being seen with him again. If she stayed away, she'd be seen anyway. The difference between a target and a bystander was posture.

She scrolled to his number, then remembered—she didn't have it. He had never given it. She had never asked. Pride or instinct, she wasn't sure which to blame.

Fine. Destiny would be arranged.

Café Bloom sat five blocks from his brownstone, neutral ground masquerading as cozy. She set up there with her laptop like any other professional woman avoiding her office. She took a table facing the door. Every few seconds, her eyes flicked to the glass, a metronome of vigilance. The air smelled like espresso and sugar; cups chimed; the world performed normality.

He arrived just before ten—no warning, no flourish, just a man ordering black coffee and stepping aside. As if she had conjured him, or as if he had been on a parallel track the whole time and the lines simply crossed.

When he turned, he spotted her immediately. His face did not change, but his step did: half a pause, then forward.

"You again," he said when he reached the table.

"You're welcome," she answered.

"For what?"

"For saving you the trouble of pretending this is coincidence."

One corner of his mouth tilted. Not quite a smile. "Are we done pretending?"

"For the next ten minutes," she said. "Sit."

He did. He didn't ask to touch the chair opposite; he didn't posture. He sat like a man used to saving his energy for what mattered.

Giselle leaned back, fingers laced loosely over the keyboard she had no intention of using. "Someone is watching me."

He absorbed the sentence without blinking. "I know."

Static roared in her ears for a beat. "You know."

"I suspected," he corrected. "I didn't know until now."

"You suspected because of you," she said. "Because proximity to you is a hazard."

"Because proximity to me draws interest," he said evenly. "Hazard is a judgment. Interest is a fact."

Her jaw tightened. "A man leaned against a lamppost across from my office. A text hit my phone inside a café I never told anyone I was in. An envelope was waiting on my desk before I arrived. If interest is a fact, we are beyond facts."

He took a slow breath, set his coffee down without drinking. "What did the envelope say?"

"You can't lock out what's already inside."

He closed his eyes for a fraction of a second, as if the sentence had a memory only, he possessed. When he opened them, they were clear. "It isn't random."

"Nothing is," she said. "Who are they?"

"The polite term is counterparties," he said. "Investors who prefer outcomes to laws. People who mistake pressure for persuasion."

"The impolite term?"

He met her gaze. "Watchers."

The word was too neat, too close to hers. A chill walked down her spine and took up residence at the base.

"Why me?" she pushed. "I am a woman you met twice who has now made the questionable decision to humor you a third time in public. Why escalate to me?"

"Because I didn't pick you up," he said. "Because you walked toward me and then away. Because they observed a variable I did not initiate and mistook you for leverage."

Giselle almost laughed; the sound would have cut skin. "So, I am a variable."

"You are the uncontrollable one," he said. "The one thing they can't put on a schedule."

She hated how much that description felt accurate and flattering at once.

"Tell me about Eva," she said, choosing the blade she wanted to test. "The journalist."

Something in his posture shifted—a half-inch of retreat no one else would have noticed. "How do you know that name?"

"Curiosity," she said. "And a friend who does not believe in coincidence."

He considered that. "Eva wrote about my family's collapse with a precision that made enemies. She was threatened. She took a leave of absence. She resurfaced in a context designed to look like a date because appearing alone would have been worse."

"Worse how?"

"Worse for her safety," he said. "I didn't like it. But I liked the alternative less."

"So you're a gentleman in public relations," Giselle said dryly. "And yet here we are, starring in a surveillance novella."

"We are here," he said, "because I stopped pretending, I could control every outcome."

That admission sounded like a truth he rarely let out of its cage. Giselle studied him for a long breath. "Who is paying for the camera outside my building?"

"I don't know," he said. "But I can know."

She weighed the hunger in his voice. Not for violence, not for theater. For information. He was not a storm; he was a barometer. He didn't chase lightning; he tracked it.

"And once you know?" she asked.

"We make terms," he said. "Or we go to ground."

"I don't do ground," she said. "I do ground rules."

His eyes warmed by a degree. "Then set one."

Her mind flicked through the frameworks she used on clients—define the objective, map the risk, assign the roles. She chose something simpler.

"No more lies," she said. "Not to me."

He didn't flinch. "Then your turn."

"For what?"

"Honesty," he said. "You ran your own check. Or your friend did. You know where I live. You know what my brother did or didn't do. You're here anyway. Why?"

Giselle could have said curiosity. She could have said boredom. She could have said the truth tastes better when it's expensive.

Instead: "Because I hate being handed a story I didn't write."

His mouth shifted again, that almost-smile. "Then write one."

"Fine," she said. "We meet in daylight, public spaces. You tell me what you know about who watches. I tell you what they've sent me. We compare notes. We decide if terms are possible."

"And if they aren't?" he asked.

She lifted her chin. "We escalate."

He nodded once, as if he'd been hoping she would say exactly that. He slid a small card across the table—no name, no logo, just a number in clean type. "Use this. Text only. If anyone else texts you from a number they claim is mine, ignore it."

Her brow arched. "Paranoid."

"Experienced," he corrected.

She took the card. The weight felt disproportionate to its size. "One more term."

"Name it."

"If you know something that puts me in the crosshairs, you tell me before I feel the heat."

His gaze held. "Agreed."

The café swell grew around them—milk steaming, spoons clinking, laughter rising and fading. For a beat, it felt almost ordinary, two people arranging the scaffolding of trust in a place built for small talk.

Her phone buzzed.

Every muscle in her body wanted to ignore it. Instead, she glanced down. An unknown number. A photo.

Her and Malcolm at the table, his hand on the card, her fingers reaching. The caption: *Terms accepted.*

Ice slid under her skin. She turned the screen so he could see. His jaw flexed once; otherwise, stillness.

"They're inside the café," she said quietly.

"Or the feed," he said. "Cameras. Reflections." He scanned the room without appearing to. "They prefer distance."

"They prefer performance," she said. "They want us to see the stage lights."

He leaned in, voice low. "Then we stop giving them clean scenes."

"How?"

"Noise," he said. "I leave first. You count to sixty, then you leave through the alley. Turn right, not left. Get in a car that isn't yours. Do not text me until you are three blocks away. Change your route twice. Delete the text with the photo. Save the number elsewhere. If they think they can choreograph us, we break the rhythm."

"I don't take choreography well," she said.

"That's why I'm suggesting and not ordering," he said. "Terms."

She wanted to argue. Instead, she nodded. "Go."

He rose without hurry, disposed of his untouched coffee, and walked out as if he were late for nothing. She forced herself to breathe the way Aunt Alicia had taught her when she was twelve and furious at a world that rewarded leaving. In for four, hold for four, out for four. She counted the seconds against the rush in her blood.

At sixty-one, she stood. She closed her laptop, slid the card into the lining of her blazer, and threaded through the tables with a smile that said she was meeting someone better elsewhere. In the hallway toward the restrooms, she took the service door and slipped into the alley that ran behind the café, the air cooler, the asphalt damp where yesterday's rain had refused to evaporate.

Turn right, he'd said. She turned right.

A rideshare idled near the dumpster, driver scrolling. She opened the door and slid in, giving an address three blocks north and two west—another café with better pastries and worse lighting. The driver nodded and pulled out.

As they merged into traffic, her phone buzzed again. Instinct said ignore; habit said control required knowledge. She looked.

Another photo. The alley, empty. Caption: *You turn right when told.*

Her mouth went dry. She deleted the message in one motion and stared straight ahead, pulse jumping in her throat. The city slid by, ordinary and monstrous.

When she stepped out three blocks later, she kept moving. Right, then left, then left again, blending into a group of shoppers, then breaking away. Only when she reached a narrow side street lined with trees did she text the number on the card.

They're closer than you think.

The dots appeared almost immediately. *I know.*

How?

Because they sent me a photo too, he replied. *Of you in the car.*

She stopped walking. The sidewalk tilted for a second and steadied. Her thumbs hovered over the glass.

Terms stand, she typed. *But understand something: I don't do victim.*

I didn't mistake you for one, he answered. *That's why they did.*

She stared at the screen until the words burned less. Then she slipped the phone into her pocket and lifted her chin. The trees shifted in a small wind. A woman laughed on a balcony three floors up. Somewhere, a siren wailed and faded.

Control is choreography, she repeated silently. But sometimes it's also improvisation.

She headed back toward the main avenue, eyes open, pace unhurried. If someone wanted a performance, they would get one. But the script would be hers.

Chapter Eleven

Lines in the Sand

The morning after Café Bloom, Giselle woke with the uneasy sense of having made a contract she hadn't signed. The card Malcolm gave her sat on her nightstand, its number clean and unyielding, like a key that opened a door she wasn't sure she wanted to enter.

She stared at it for a long time before moving, fingers itching to text and demand answers. But control meant patience. If she had learned anything from men who thought they could keep her, it was that hunger was weakness. She would not be the first to flinch.

Instead, she moved through her routine with precision. Shower scalding, eyeliner sharp, blazer a shade of navy that announced authority without begging for it. She poured herself coffee strong enough to disguise exhaustion and stood at her window overlooking the street below.

Normal morning life hummed there—parents tugging at kids' hands, joggers panting past, a delivery man balancing boxes. And yet she couldn't unsee the shape of watchers in all of them. The man pausing too long at the corner. The woman scrolling a phone without looking down. Her mind turned every stranger into a spy.

She told herself that was paranoia. Then she remembered the photo of her in the car. Not paranoia. Confirmation.

By ten, she was in the office, pushing through client meetings with a sharp smile. She adjusted logos, pitched campaigns, smoothed over egos. But every screen felt like a potential mirror, every email like

67

a trick. When her assistant mentioned a courier had dropped off a package, Giselle's pulse spiked before she saw it was just a box of sample lipsticks.

The watchers had already taught her: fear is cumulative.

By lunch, she gave up on pretending she wasn't waiting. She pulled out the card, stared at the number. The rules were simple: text only. Nothing traceable.

She typed: *We need to meet. Neutral ground. My terms.*

Seconds stretched, long enough she thought maybe he would ignore her. Then dots appeared.

When?

Tonight.

Where?

She hesitated. Naming a place meant conceding control. But control was choreography—she reminded herself again—and choreography meant sometimes you chose the stage.

Glass House rooftop. Seven.

The Glass House was a bar built for people who wanted to be seen but not touched, all glass walls and mirrored ceilings, rooftop seating that glittered against the skyline. Public enough to feel safe. Controlled enough to feel intentional.

His reply came quick. *Agreed.*

No emoji. No flourish. Just that.

She slipped the card back into her bag, heart thudding harder than she wanted to admit.

By seven, the rooftop gleamed under a bruised sunset. The skyline glittered like teeth, and the air carried the crisp bite of early autumn. Giselle arrived in black—a dress that whispered danger without shouting it. Her heels clicked against the glass floor as if marking territory.

Malcolm was already there. Of course, he was. Leaning against the railing, glass of water in hand, as if alcohol was a luxury he couldn't afford.

"You're early," she said, sliding into the chair opposite.

"You're late," he countered, glancing at his watch. "By two minutes."

"Fashionably," she said, forcing ease.

He studied her for a moment, then nodded toward the server who appeared silently. She ordered wine; he kept his water.

"You chose the stage," he said once they were alone again.

"Which makes me director," she said. "So answer the question: who exactly are they?"

His jaw flexed. "Counterparties, like I told you. Offshore money tied to my brother's mess. When I pulled the thread, they noticed. They've been watching ever since."

"And Eva?" she pressed.

"Eva wrote too close to the truth. She was pressured off the record. I tried to protect her, but protection has limits." His voice softened, barely audible over the city hum. "Limits you don't understand until you hit them."

Something in his eyes flickered then, a weight she didn't want to carry but couldn't look away from.

"So why me?" she demanded. "Why the photos, the texts? What do I have to do with your collapse?"

"You don't," he said. "Not yet. Which is why they're using you. Pressure works better when it's indirect."

Her laugh came sharp, dangerous. "So, I'm a pawn."

His gaze didn't waver. "No. You're bait."

The word landed like glass shattering between them.

She leaned back, crossing her legs. "Bait bites back."

"I know," he said simply.

She hated that answer, hated how steady he sounded.

"Then here are my rules," she said, voice low. "You keep me informed. No more half-truths. If I'm in their crosshairs, I want to see the barrel before it fires."

He inclined his head. "Agreed."

"And if they come too close—" She stopped, throat tightening, the image of that envelope flashing in her mind. "We don't wait. We hit back."

A silence stretched. Then, slowly, he nodded.

The server returned with her wine, interrupting the gravity for a moment. Giselle sipped, savoring the burn. Across from her, Malcolm drank his water like ritual.

"You don't scare easily," he said finally.

"I scare constantly," she admitted. "I just don't let it win."

For the first time, something like respect softened his features. "Then maybe we can write a story that ends differently."

The words unsettled her more than any threat. Because for the briefest moment, she wanted to believe him.

Later, when she left the Glass House alone, she felt eyes again. Not his. Not strangers. Something colder.

Her phone buzzed before she reached the street.

Another photo.

Her and Malcolm on the rooftop, wine glass midair, his face turned toward hers.

Caption: *Beautiful view.*

Her breath caught. The photo was taken from above—from a drone or a building across the street.

She deleted it quickly, but her hand shook. The watchers weren't just close. They were above, around, everywhere.

And for the first time, she realized something terrifying: she wasn't sure if Malcolm was her ally… or if sitting beside him had just painted a brighter target on her back.

Chapter Thirteen

Unwelcome Echoes

Giselle woke with the taste of adrenaline still sharp in her mouth. The text from the night before sat burned into her mind, the silhouette of herself framed in Malcolm's doorway, captioned like a cruel joke. She had deleted it within seconds, but deletion didn't erase the image. It lingered in her body, a heaviness in her chest she couldn't shake.

She dressed slowly that morning, dragging her routine out longer than usual, not because she was tired but because she dreaded the quiet that followed when she was ready too early. Silence gave the watchers more room to breathe. She pulled on a fitted gray dress, looped on gold earrings, painted her mouth crimson. By the time she looked in the mirror, her reflection was flawless, but the perfection felt brittle, like glass waiting for a crack.

At the office, she tried to lose herself in the day. Clients demanded everything as usual: impossible deadlines, dazzling campaigns, miracles performed with slides and slogans. Normally, Giselle thrived on the pressure. Today, it pressed differently. She caught herself checking the blinds more often, scanning reflections in glass walls, looking for shadows where none should be. Her assistant asked if she was alright. Giselle said yes, because what else could she say?

By lunch she couldn't sit still. She texted Serena: *Dinner tonight. No arguments.*

Serena responded within seconds: *Finally. You're buying.*

The hours crawled until evening. Giselle closed her laptop and slipped into the city's night air, heels tapping rhythm against concrete, neon signs painting her skin. Serena chose a noisy restaurant where the tables were too close together and the air buzzed with conversation. Perfect. Too much noise for anyone to listen clearly.

"You look like hell," Serena said when Giselle slid into the booth.

"And you look like a woman who should be more grateful for free food," Giselle countered, summoning a smirk.

Serena wasn't fooled. She leaned forward, lowering her voice under the cover of laughter from the next table. "It's worse, isn't it?"

Giselle toyed with the stem of her wine glass. "They sent another photo."

Serena's expression hardened. "Of what?"

"Me. In Malcolm's doorway."

Serena swore under her breath. "They're close."

"They've always been close," Giselle said. "Now they're showing me how close."

Serena studied her, the usual teasing edge gone. "You can't do this alone. You're strong, yes, but strength doesn't stop cameras. Doesn't stop whoever is behind them."

"And Malcolm does?"

"Does he?" Serena asked back.

The question sank deeper than Giselle wanted it to. She didn't answer.

Dinner passed with half-hearted jokes and muted laughter, but beneath it all lay the same question Serena had voiced: was Malcolm part of the solution, or the problem in disguise?

Back at her loft later that night, Giselle poured herself a drink and sat by the window, watching the city pulse. For a long time nothing moved, nothing shifted. Just cars passing, people walking, the endless theater of a city that never rested. She almost convinced herself the watchers had grown bored.

Then her phone buzzed.

No photo this time. Just a line of text: *You trust the wrong people.*

Her throat tightened. She stared at the words until her reflection blurred in the glass.

Who? Malcolm? Serena? Herself?

Before she could think too hard, she typed back: *If you know so much, come out of the shadows. Stop hiding.*

The reply came almost instantly. *Shadows are safer. For you. For me.*

She deleted the thread, though her body remembered every letter. Then she set her phone face down and forced herself to breathe. Control is choreography, she told herself again, but the dance felt different now, as if someone else had already written the steps.

The next morning she forced herself into routine again. By mid-afternoon, a courier arrived at her office with a small white box tied in string. No sender, no markings.

Her assistant carried it in. "It was left downstairs. No signature."

Giselle dismissed her quickly, pulse racing. She stared at the box for a long minute before finally pulling the string loose.

Inside was a single chess piece: a black queen.

No note.

Her breath caught. She lifted it out, its weight solid in her hand, heavier than she expected. She hated the implication. Pawns, bait, now a queen. Someone was playing a game and had just told her she was the centerpiece.

That night she found herself standing outside Malcolm's brownstone again, the queen in her coat pocket like a secret she hadn't decided how to share.

When he opened the door, he looked at her as if he'd been expecting her. "You shouldn't be here."

"I know," she said. "But here I am."

She stepped inside without waiting, pulled the queen from her pocket, and set it on the table between them.

His expression didn't change, but something flickered in his eyes. Recognition.

"They know what you are," he said quietly.

"And what am I?"

He looked at her, steady and unflinching. "The piece they'll sacrifice everything else to capture."

Her pulse hammered, but her smile didn't falter. "Then let's make sure they regret trying."

Chapter Fourteen

Countermoves

Giselle didn't sleep. She lay on her back and stared at the ceiling until dawn thinned the room into something gentler than night. The chess queen sat on the dresser where she'd placed it, a dark silhouette against the pale wall, watching her like an accusation. She refused to put it back in the box. A box implied ownership. She would not live inside anyone's container.

At seven, she showered, dressed, pinned up her hair, and slipped the queen into her coat pocket. She didn't know why she brought it. Maybe as a reminder. Maybe as a dare. Outside, the city had that fragile, washed-clean feeling that lasted exactly ten minutes before the day dirtied it again. She moved fast. She needed a plan that wasn't just reaction wearing a prettier name.

Malcolm answered her text before the bubbles could finish pulsing: *Come by. Ten minutes.*

When he opened the brownstone door, he didn't greet her. He stepped back so she could pass, then locked three different deadbolts with the kind of precision that made her stomach tighten. The lemon-and-paper smell again. The neatness that felt like restraint, not taste. He nodded toward the kitchen. "Coffee?"

"Strategy," she said, then softened the edge. "And coffee."

He poured for both of them without asking how she took it. Black, because he remembered. A small mercy. She set the queen on the

77

table between them like evidence. His eyes flicked to it and away. He didn't touch it.

"They chose the right piece," he said.

"They chose the loudest one," she countered. "What would they have sent you?"

"Not a piece," he said. "A board."

The answer made something tighten low in her chest. "Meaning?"

"Meaning they believe I keep track of rules other people pretend don't exist."

"Do you?"

"Yes," he said simply. "Because people who forget rules usually belong to someone else's."

She sipped her coffee. "I want to break their game."

"That requires naming it," he said. "Two fronts: pressure and narrative. They pressure you. They manage perception so you question your own."

"And you?"

"They watch to learn who I will protect," he said. "They expect I'll make mistakes in that direction."

Her mouth curved without humor. "They expect you to choose me."

"They expect I already did," he said, steady as a verdict.

The admission landed with a heat she refused to show. She placed her fingertips on the table to keep from clenching her hands. "Then we give them a mistake to misread."

"We need noise," he agreed. "Patterns they can't map."

"I'm good at noise," she said. "But it needs to mean something." She tapped the queen. "I want them to move first and regret it."

He held her gaze. "There's a woman you need to meet."

"Eva," she said.

He nodded once. "She won't like it. But she understands the watchers better than anyone who's still above ground."

"Where?"

"A place that pretends to be public and is actually private," he said. "She consults mornings for a nonprofit two neighborhoods over. If I call, she won't answer. If I appear, she'll leave. If you appear with me, she'll decide we're either foolish or serious."

Giselle stood. "Let's be serious."

They left together, not touching, not speaking except to agree on the route that doubled back twice and cut through a farmers market where the crowd masked their angles. At the nonprofit—a dull brick building with a cheerful hand-painted sign—Malcolm buzzed a side door. A camera blinked. The lock clicked.

The woman who opened it had lipstick as sharp as a blade and eyes that gave nothing away. Eva was beautiful in the way danger sometimes is: more shape than color, more line than curve. She looked Giselle up and down once, then ignored her entirely and addressed Malcolm. "Do you enjoy breaking my rules?"

"You change them too often to memorize," he said, voice even.

"Because you force me to," she said, then stepped back. "Ten minutes."

Her office was small, shelves crowded with reports and framed headlines cut off at their edges. It smelled like paper and a woman who keeps her promises even when she shouldn't. Eva sat, gestured to the two chairs that didn't match. Giselle took the one with a loose arm and crossed her legs like she had never known discomfort.

"You brought her," Eva said to Malcolm without looking at Giselle. "So the watchers brought her too."

Giselle answered before Malcolm could. "They were always going to. The question is whether they win with it."

Eva's gaze shifted. Appraisal. "Are you brave or tired?"

"Depends who's asking," Giselle replied.

Something like approval flickered in Eva's eyes and vanished. "State your problem in a sentence."

"They know where I am before I do," Giselle said.

"And yours?" Eva asked Malcolm.

"They want to use her to flush me," he said.

Eva leaned back. "Then stop running like the fox and start running like the hounds."

Giselle frowned. "Meaning?"

"You're trying to predict where they'll strike," Eva said. "That assumes a single hand. There isn't one. There's a network anchored by two or three nodes with separate appetites. The photos are one node—voyeurs who love theater. The texts are another—handlers who test compliance. The gifts are a third—someone who wants you to play a role."

"The queen," Giselle said, tapping her pocket unconsciously.

Eva nodded. "They're telling you what they want you to be. Queens are powerful and stationary. They want you visible, central, predictable. Don't be."

Malcolm's jaw tightened. "We thought noise—breaking their rhythm."

"Noise is useful," Eva said. "But noise without narrative looks like panic. Give them a story that maps to your noise. Something plausible. Something they want to believe."

Giselle's mind shifted into the gear she used on clients: desire, fear, promise. She breathed once, slow. "If they want me central, give them central—on my terms. Announce a public campaign. A brand launch. Something that puts me everywhere and nowhere at once. Cameras will find me because I will already be in cameras."

Eva's eyes warmed a degree. "Better. But you need a reason to be everywhere."

"A client with money and nerves," Giselle said. "Which I can have by Wednesday."

Malcolm glanced at her. "You can?"

"I make people interesting for a living," she said. "Fame is a faucet. The trick is not drowning."

Eva tapped a pen against the desk. "I'll do one better. I'll leak that a certain investment-adjacent nonprofit—ours—is launching a campaign on financial harm and coercion. We'll say we hired your firm to design it. We'll say you're building a storytelling series featuring survivors. It gives you movement without needing an excuse. It gives your movement a moral spine that makes you harder to attack in daylight."

Giselle almost smiled. "And it draws them because they hate scrutiny dressed as virtue."

"Exactly," Eva said. "They'll have to decide whether to follow you into rooms with witnesses or wait outside and risk losing the thread."

"And while we move," Malcolm said, "we watch back."

Eva slid a small device from her drawer. "Detector. Not perfect, but it screams at most common wireless bugs. Keep it on you. And if your phone pings from a number that looks familiar, assume it's a copycat until I say otherwise. I'll send you a secure channel later." She paused. "Don't post anything you can't live with on a courtroom screen."

Giselle took the device, felt its cheap, promising weight. "Thank you," she said, meaning it more than she expected.

Eva looked past her to Malcolm. "Keep her in front of you, not behind. If she's in your shadow, they'll decide you care. If she leads, they'll doubt."

He nodded. "We know how to stage."

"Do you?" Eva's voice softened, not kind, not cruel. "Because they do theatre for a living. They see light differently than you think. Ten minutes are up."

Outside, the sky had tilted toward noon. Giselle and Malcolm stepped into the brightness without touching. When they were half a block away, she exhaled the breath she hadn't noticed she'd been holding.

"She trusts you," Giselle said.

"She distrusts me consistently," he corrected. "It looks like trust because it doesn't change when she likes me."

"That's a kind of love," Giselle said, only half mocking.

The corner of his mouth moved. "For some people."

They cut south two blocks, then doubled back north, crossed at a light, and flowed into pedestrian traffic like a sentence finishing itself. Giselle kept her gaze high, face calm, thoughts moving between the intel and its implications. Queens are powerful and stationary. Don't be. She would not be anyone's statue.

By late afternoon, she had a preliminary campaign deck in her inbox from her design lead, who could build a cathedral from a napkin sketch if she believed in the idea. Giselle spent an hour sharpening language, another choosing images that said survivor instead of victim. She wrote a statement for the nonprofit in a voice that wasn't hers and yet fit in her mouth like something she'd been waiting to say: *When money hides harm, stories become flashlights.*

At five, she stepped onto the street for air. A woman with a stroller passed. A bike courier whistled by, tires whispering. A man she might have recognized from yesterday leaned against a parking meter and looked past her, through her, like she was the glass he wanted to see beyond. It didn't matter. Let him watch. Let him report that the queen had left the board and taken the street.

Her phone buzzed. A message from an unknown number: *We see you working.*

She typed back: *You'll need to see faster.*

No response. Good. Let silence be the noise for once.

At seven, Serena appeared at her office door with a bag of takeout and an expression that said she was prepared to stage an intervention. "If you don't feed yourself, I will file a complaint with HR."

"I am HR," Giselle said.

"Exactly," Serena said, dropping the bag. Her eyes narrowed at the detector on the desk. "What fresh toy is that?"

"Insurance," Giselle said. She explained the nonprofit, the campaign, the plan that was more scaffolding than structure. As she spoke, Serena's posture shifted from skeptical to energized, the way it always did when a mess became a project.

"This is reckless," Serena concluded, "and also the correct amount of petty." She grinned. "I'll help. But if I end up on a billboard as the face of cautionary tales, I will end you."

Giselle felt something she hadn't in days: a small, warm lift under the ribs. "Deal."

They ate at her table like they had when they were broke and building things from air. Serena told a story about a client who wanted her to plan a birthday party with a theme of "quiet opulence," and for five minutes they laughed like women not currently negotiating with an invisible chorus.

Giselle's phone buzzed again. This time, a photo. Not of her. Not of Malcolm. A tight shot of a hand placing a chess queen on a marble table. Caption: *Your move.*

She didn't delete it. She saved it and forwarded it to the secure channel Eva had texted an hour earlier. Then she turned the detector on and swept the office. It hummed only at the window—no shock there—then quieted. Good enough for now.

At nine, after Serena left with a mock salute and three warnings, Giselle stood alone at the window and watched the city's late lights blink awake. She thought of queens and boards, of foxes and hounds, of noise and narrative. She thought of Eva's face when she said don't be stationary. She thought of Malcolm's steady agreement to rules most people would have tried to charm their way around.

She slipped the chess queen from her pocket, set it on the windowsill, and turned it so it faced the street. She didn't know if any camera could catch the angle. She didn't care.

"I'm not your piece," she said into the glass, into the city, into the small, attentive dark. "I'm the player you forgot exists."

Her phone vibrated. This time, it was Malcolm: *Tomorrow. Ten. Same place as before. We shift routes after.*

She typed back: *Bring a board.*

I'll bring a timer, he replied.

Giselle smiled, the first true one in days. Control wasn't a box, and it wasn't a mask. It was a set of choices made in sequence, on purpose, while someone else expected you to flinch. She shut off the lights, left the queen facing the street, and walked out of her office carrying the narrative in one hand and the detector in the other. The night met her like a stage with the curtain already lifted.

If the watchers wanted theatre, she would give them a play that burned down the house.

Chapter Fifteen

Smoke and Mirrors

Giselle arrived at Café Bloom early the next morning, the queen still in her pocket, its weight a reminder and a provocation. She had promised herself she wouldn't let it define her, but carrying it kept the fear from looking too large. If she was the queen, she would also be the hand that moved it.

The café buzzed with its usual chaos: students hunched over laptops, couples leaning in over croissants, the hiss and pop of the espresso machine like background percussion. She chose a seat near the window, her back to the wall, every angle accounted for. Control wasn't just a word—it was placement.

Malcolm entered five minutes later, punctual as ever. He wore a charcoal jacket, same as the day before, the kind of consistency that spoke of routine rather than vanity. His eyes swept the room once, quick, subtle, cataloging exits and faces before landing on her.

"You're early," he said as he sat.

"You're predictable," she returned, sliding the queen onto the table between them.

He glanced at it but didn't touch. "Did they send another?"

"Last night." She kept her voice low, steady. "A photo of a hand placing a queen on marble. Caption: *Your move.*"

His jaw tightened almost imperceptibly. "They want escalation."

85

"Then let's escalate," she said.

He studied her for a long moment. "Careful. Escalation is oxygen to them."

"And fear is oxygen to me," she replied. "We all breathe something."

The server interrupted with their drinks—her usual cappuccino, his black coffee. The clatter of cups gave them cover, and Giselle leaned closer once the server left.

"Eva's idea works," she said. "A campaign. Noise with narrative. But noise won't save us unless we control the mirrors too."

"Mirrors?"

She tapped the window with one manicured nail. "Every reflection they use to catch us. Every surface that can be turned into proof. We flip it. We create reflections of our own."

He leaned back, expression unreadable but listening.

"You want to smoke them out," he said at last.

"I want to confuse them," she corrected. "If they think they're watching me, I want them to question which me they're watching. If they see us together, I want them to wonder if it's staged. If they capture my face, I want them to wonder if I intended it."

Malcolm's mouth tilted slightly. "Deception as defense."

"Perception as power," she countered.

For a moment, his eyes warmed, a flash of approval she hadn't realized she wanted.

"Then we need allies," he said. "You can stage narrative. I can track nodes. Eva can map the web. But three people won't outmaneuver a network."

"Who else?"

"People who owe me," he said simply. "Some don't like me. But they dislike the watchers more."

"And they'll risk it?"

"They already risked everything once. This is just choosing a side again."

She considered him for a long moment, weighing the gamble. He might be recruiting ghosts or he might be inviting wolves to dinner. But wolves still had teeth, and teeth had uses.

"Fine," she said. "Bring them in. But my rule stands—no shadows. If they want to help, they do it in daylight, where I can see their faces."

He nodded once. "Agreed."

A man at the counter dropped his change. The coins scattered, one rolling under their table. Giselle's hand darted down to retrieve it, but her fingers brushed against something else instead—a folded scrap of paper tucked beneath the chair.

She froze, then unfolded it slowly. Six words written in block letters: *Queens fall when pawns betray first.*

She handed it to Malcolm. His expression didn't change, but his eyes hardened.

"They were here before us," he said quietly.

"Or sitting among us," she murmured, scanning the room. Too many faces. Too much noise. Any one of them could have placed it.

Her chest tightened, but she forced her shoulders back. "Let them watch," she said, tucking the note into her pocket with the queen. "But they'll choke on the story I give them."

That evening, Giselle threw herself into the campaign with a ferocity that startled even her. She summoned her design team, pushed them harder than ever, demanded visuals that screamed resilience instead of pity. Words mattered, images mattered, every shade of color mattered. She stripped out anything that smelled of victimhood. What remained was sharp, modern, undeniable.

By ten p.m., the first mock-ups glowed across the screen: *When money hides harm, stories become flashlights.* The line Eva had suggested, dressed now in bold typography and framed by stark portraits. Not models. Real faces from stock images she'd twisted until they felt raw.

Her team left exhausted but buzzing, the kind of late-night high that comes when creation feels urgent. Giselle stayed behind, staring at the screen long after they'd gone. The images looked back at her, daring her to believe in her own strength.

Her phone buzzed. A new message, no number.

A photo of her campaign mock-up.

Caption: *You write, we read.*

Her hands tightened around the phone. She should have been furious. Instead, she felt something sharper—acknowledgment. They weren't mocking. They were watching closer now, paying attention. And attention could be used.

She typed back: *Then read carefully.*

No response.

She leaned back, exhaling. Smoke and mirrors, she thought. If they wanted a queen, she would be a queen. But one they couldn't predict, one they couldn't corner.

By midnight, she was still awake, drafting speeches in her head, rehearsing glances, practicing smiles that meant one thing on camera and another off it. Every move choreographed, every gesture loaded. If control was theatre, then she was the lead actress now, and the watchers would not know which act was real until the curtain fell.

The chess queen sat on her desk beside the note. Together, they looked less like threats and more like props.

And Giselle decided she would learn to direct the play.

Chapter Sixteen

The Leak

By morning, Giselle's campaign had teeth. Eva's nonprofit issued the first press release at eight a.m., and within two hours three blogs had reposted it. By noon, a business journal had run a headline: *Brand Strategist Giselle Laurent Leads Bold Campaign on Financial Harm.* The article included her headshot, cropped from an old interview, eyes sharp and defiant above a caption that suddenly felt prophetic.

She read it twice, sipping her coffee, and realized the watchers would see the same lines she did. Her face was public now, her name threaded into a narrative about power and scrutiny. Eva had been right—it made her harder to touch in daylight.

Her phone buzzed before she could close the tab. A text from the secure channel: *Good coverage. Stay visible. Don't overplay it.* Eva again.

Another message followed seconds later, this one from an unknown number: *Visibility makes you vulnerable.*

Giselle deleted it before it could burrow into her chest. Vulnerability wasn't weakness, not when it was chosen. She would own this campaign so completely that the watchers couldn't weaponize it.

At the office, her team was electric. Designers plastered screens with mockups, copywriters spun headlines, interns ran coffee like adrenaline shots. The energy reminded Giselle of her early days— building a name out of grit and charm, living on the edge of collapse and triumph. For a few hours, she almost forgot the shadows.

Almost.

By mid-afternoon, Malcolm appeared in her doorway. He didn't text ahead, didn't ask permission. He simply walked in, steady and quiet, carrying his presence like armor. Her assistant stared, wide-eyed, but Giselle waved her off.

"You've made news," he said.

"Eva moves fast," she replied.

"And you look like a woman who hasn't eaten since yesterday."

She gestured toward the desk piled with takeout containers. "Evidence to the contrary."

He smiled faintly, the closest thing he had to warmth. Then his expression shifted. "We need to talk. Not here."

"Why not here?"

He stepped closer, lowering his voice. "Because your office is compromised."

Her pulse jumped. "How do you know?"

He pulled a small device from his pocket—the detector Eva had given them, upgraded with modifications she didn't recognize. He swept it across the room. It stayed quiet until it passed near the vent above her desk. The device squealed, a shrill, piercing sound.

Giselle's stomach dropped.

"They planted a mic," Malcolm said flatly.

She forced herself to remain calm, though her throat felt tight. "How long?"

"No way to know. Days. Weeks."

Her fists clenched. Someone had been listening, watching her run her empire, hearing every late-night call, every vulnerable word. Fury burned hotter than fear.

"Then let's give them something to hear," she said.

He looked at her, steady. "Careful."

"No," she said. "Strategic."

She turned to her team, her mask flawless. "Everyone, pack up. Work remote for the rest of the week. I need the space."

No one questioned her. Within minutes the office emptied, leaving her alone with Malcolm and the hum of the city outside.

She set the queen on the desk directly beneath the vent. "Let's play to the audience."

Malcolm folded his arms. "What do you propose?"

"A fight," she said. "Loud, believable, messy. Something they can record and misinterpret."

He didn't argue. Instead, he leaned against the desk, eyes narrowing. "You're reckless."

"You're secretive," she shot back. "You've pulled me into a game without telling me the rules. And now my office is bugged because of you."

His tone sharpened. "Because you chose proximity."

Her voice rose, echoing off the glass walls. "Because you lied by omission. Because you let me walk into danger blind. Because you think control is silence when control is narrative."

He stepped closer, voice low but sharp enough to cut. "You think you're the only one rewriting the story? I've been playing survival while you've been playing theatre."

"And maybe I'll survive because I make theatre," she snapped.

They stared at each other, fury staged but not entirely false. The air between them hummed. She turned sharply, heels striking against the floor, and slammed her bag shut with a sound that rang through the room.

"Get out," she said coldly.

For a moment, silence. Then he walked to the door, his movements deliberate, heavy enough to be heard through a microphone. He paused with his hand on the handle, voice like stone. "Careful what you wish for."

The door clicked shut behind him.

Giselle exhaled slowly, chest tight. The fight had been staged, yes—but it had scraped raw truths in the process. Still, it was a performance, and performances had power. If the watchers thought cracks were forming, they might reposition, show themselves, make mistakes.

Her phone buzzed minutes later. An unknown number again.

Arguments are dangerous. Queens lose allies first.

She smiled faintly, controlled, defiant. She typed back: *Or they make pawns overconfident.*

No reply came. But silence was its own answer.

That night, she met Malcolm two blocks from her loft, in the shadow of a closed bookstore. He was waiting, hands in his pockets, expression unreadable.

"They believed it," he said quietly.

"They always believe what they want to," she answered.

He studied her for a moment. "And what do you want them to believe?"

She held his gaze. "That I'm two moves ahead."

His eyes softened briefly, then hardened again. "Then let's make sure you are."

The city moved around them, ordinary and oblivious. But Giselle knew better. Somewhere, someone had listened to every word, every breath. And if they wanted a queen cornered, they had chosen the wrong woman.

Chapter Seventeen

Fault Lines

Giselle woke before dawn, her body still buzzing from the staged fight in her office. She replayed it over and over in her head, Malcolm's sharp words, her own cutting replies. Some of it had been performance. Some of it hadn't. That was the part that unsettled her most.

She pulled the queen from her nightstand and set it on the counter while she made coffee. The piece gleamed faintly in the early light, a reminder that everything now was theatre, even her silence. She would not let the watchers decide what role she played.

By the time she reached her office, her team was already online, sending her drafts, design tweaks, and frantic late-night brainstorms. She responded to each with precision. No one sensed the vent above her desk was compromised, that every word yesterday had been a performance meant for ears not present. That was her secret to manage.

At noon, Serena stormed in with a bag of takeout.

"You're impossible," Serena said, dropping the food on the desk. "You vanish, you don't answer, and then I hear rumors your office is going remote because of 'renovations.' What's happening?"

Giselle offered a smile she didn't feel. "We needed a refresh. New energy."

"Lies," Serena said flatly. "You've got that look again—the one you had when Troy broke your heart and you swore you'd never cry over a man again. Except this time it's bigger than heartbreak."

Giselle didn't answer. She opened the takeout container instead, the smell of sesame and garlic spilling into the room.

Serena sat, eyes narrowing. "It's Malcolm, isn't it? He's trouble. I told you."

"It's not Malcolm," Giselle said, too sharp.

Serena tilted her head. "Then what?"

"Someone's watching," Giselle admitted before she could stop herself. "Bugged my office. Following me. Sending photos."

Serena froze, her bravado cracking. "Why didn't you tell me sooner?"

"Because you'd worry. Because you'd tell me to run."

"Because you should run," Serena snapped.

"I don't run," Giselle said coldly.

The silence between them stretched, brittle and dangerous. Then Serena sighed, leaning back. "Fine. If you won't run, at least let me help."

Giselle softened, just slightly. "You already are."

That evening, she met Malcolm again, this time in the lobby of a hotel where neither of them were staying. The space buzzed with tourists and business travelers, the kind of noise that swallowed conversation whole.

"You were right," he said as soon as they sat. "The fight worked. They shifted. Eva traced a ping back to an IP cluster in the docks district. It's sloppy, but it's something."

"Sloppy means intentional," Giselle said. "They want us to see it."

"Or they want to test whether we're watching back."

Her eyes narrowed. "Then let's pass the test."

He studied her, steady and unreadable. "You're enjoying this."

"I'm alive in this," she corrected. "There's a difference."

His silence said more than words. He didn't approve, but he understood.

A server passed with a tray of drinks. For a moment, Giselle's eyes followed the reflection in the polished surface, scanning faces behind her. Two men lingered near the bar, pretending to argue over a bill. One woman sat alone, her eyes flicking to them too often. The watchers weren't subtle tonight.

"They want us to know they're here," she murmured.

"Yes," Malcolm said. "And that means they want something."

Her phone buzzed. Another message, no number. *Queens break when their pawns lie.*

She showed him the screen. "They're trying to fracture us."

"They'll fail if we decide otherwise," he said.

She looked at him for a long moment. "Do you trust me?"

"Yes," he said without hesitation.

Her throat tightened. "Then I'll trust you back. But if you ever lie to me again—"

"I won't," he said. His voice was steady, but there was something in his eyes—regret, maybe, or the shadow of something unsaid.

The moment stretched between them, fragile as glass

Later, she walked home alone, deliberately slow, every sense alive. Halfway down her block, she felt it again—that itch of eyes, the weight of attention pressing on her skin. She turned sharply, scanning the street. Nothing obvious. No shadow she could pin down.

But when she reached her building, the doorman handed her an envelope. "Left for you, Ms. Laurent."

Her pulse quickened as she slit it open. Inside was another photo—this time of Serena, leaving Giselle's office earlier that day with the takeout bag.

The caption: *Pawns wander too close to the board.*

For the first time, fear cut deeper than anger. This wasn't about her anymore.

She dialed Serena immediately. "Where are you?"

"At home, why?"

"Stay there. Don't leave. Lock your doors."

Serena's voice sharpened. "What's going on?"

"I'll explain later. Just do it."

She hung up before Serena could argue, her hand trembling.

The watchers had widened the field. And now, the cost of every move was no longer hers alone to pay.

Chapter Eighteen

Collateral

Giselle did not sleep. Fear had a new shape now, not the sharp, metallic taste she carried alone but something wider, heavier—a net thrown over the people she loved. She paced her loft until the city softened from black to bruised blue. At five a.m., she texted Serena again. *Still safe?*

A minute later: *Yes. Doors locked. You're scaring me, G.*

Good, Giselle typed. *Be scared enough to listen. I'll send a car at eight. Come to my place. Not your usual route.*

Serena's typing dots appeared, disappeared, then returned. *Bossy.* Then: *Fine.*

Giselle pressed her hands to her eyes until fireworks sparked. Anger steadied her breathing. Anger had edges she could hold. She showered, dressed in black trousers and a slate blouse, braided her hair tight like a promise. By the time Serena arrived—hood up, sunglasses on despite the early light—Giselle had coffee waiting and a plan stacked in bullet points on a legal pad.

Serena dropped onto the couch and eyed the pad. "You made an agenda for terror."

"I made choices," Giselle said. "We stick to them."

Serena's humor drained. "Show me."

Giselle walked her through it: Eva's intel, the staged fight, the confirmed bug in the office vent, the IP cluster in the docks district. Serena listened without interrupting, jaw set, fingers tight around her mug.

When she finished, Serena blew out a long breath. "Okay. First of all, I hate men with hobbies. Second, you should've told me sooner. Third, I'm in."

"You're not in," Giselle said. "You're safe. Different things."

Serena shook her head. "I'm in."

Love, Giselle thought grimly, always insisted on being useful. "Then you follow orders."

"I follow plans," Serena said. "And you follow mine when they're better."

Giselle didn't argue. "Fine. We start by moving the campaign launch up. Today at five. Not Thursday. Public venue, cameras, witnesses."

"Where?"

"City Arts Hall."

Serena blinked. "You can't book that in a day."

"I just did," Giselle said, holding up her phone. "Favors. Money helps."

Serena laughed despite the tension. "Of course you did."

By noon, journalists had confirmed attendance, council aides RSVP'd, and the hall's coordinator had agreed to a three o'clock staging call. The machine of visibility whirred to life, loud and blessedly predictable.

At one, a courier buzzed. Serena tensed. Giselle opened the door to a florist's box—white, expensive, ribboned like a threat. She carried it to the kitchen island and slit it open.

Inside lay a single white lily, huge and perfect, its scent already too sweet. Beneath it, a glossy card: *Condolences.*

Serena swore. "They're disgusting."

"They're dramatic," Giselle corrected, sliding the card into a baggie for Eva. She tossed the flower into the trash. She snapped a photo and texted it: *Docks node getting theatrical.*

Eva's reply came fast: *They want you rattled. You just balanced. Keep moving. FYI: cluster went quiet at 12:17. Relocation or restraint.*

Or they're coming to the show, Giselle typed.

Assume they're already seated, Eva answered.

At three, Giselle and Serena arrived at the Arts Hall. The atrium's glass walls poured light over the space, the black-box theater humming with workers adjusting chairs and microphones. Visibility was architecture here.

Malcolm was already inside, conferring with security. He met Giselle with steady eyes. "Entrances monitored, service hall blocked. Cameras cover lobby and stage. Eva's team swept twice. No bugs."

"No visible bugs," Serena muttered.

Giselle set the queen on the lectern, half ritual, half reminder.

The stage manager walked them through cues: Giselle's remarks, a survivor montage, Eva's panel, Q&A. It was work, familiar and grounding. When the first press badge flashed at the door, adrenaline settled into Giselle's veins like clarity.

By five, the hall filled—journalists, nonprofit staff, curious public. Serena took up a position by the aisle like a sentinel. Malcolm stood at the back, presence quiet but heavy. Eva arrived brisk, notes in hand, tote on her shoulder, eyes sharp as ever.

"You've done more in a day than most campaigns do in a quarter," she told Giselle. "Good. Now glide, don't sprint."

"I plan to," Giselle said.

The montage played. Faces and voices wove into a message: money can be a weapon; stories can be armor. When the lights rose, Giselle walked to the lectern with the queen in her pocket.

She began without preamble. She spoke of coercion and visibility, of shame growing in darkness and transparency as bleach. She didn't say watchers. She didn't need to. The room listened.

Halfway through, her phone buzzed twice in her blazer. She ignored it until the applause came, then slipped to the wings.

A text. Unknown number. A photo of the lobby: Serena speaking with a man in a navy suit. Caption: *Pawns change sides.*

Giselle's stomach knotted. She zoomed in. Serena's smile was polite, but her body leaned away. She was managing him, not welcoming him.

Giselle texted Malcolm: *Navy suit. Lobby. Watcher energy.*

From the back, Malcolm angled toward the lobby. Giselle watched from the wings as the man handed Serena a card. She didn't take it. Malcolm did. Whatever he saw made his eyes narrow. He pocketed the card, spoke low, and the man lifted his hands like surrender before slipping into the street.

Malcolm snapped a photo of the card and sent it to Eva. Seconds later, he texted Giselle: *Dock address. 8 pm. Tonight.*

She stared at the time. Six forty-five.

Trap or invitation? she typed.

Both, he answered. *We take witnesses.*

Eva found her in the wings. Giselle showed her the text. Eva's mouth tightened. "They want to move you from light to dark before the glow fades."

"Then we carry light," Giselle said. "We record everything."

"They'll jam signals," Eva warned.

"Then we upload later. Either way, we control first narrative."

Eva agreed with a single nod.

At seven fifteen, after the panel, Giselle gave closing remarks. She ended on an unplanned line: "Stories don't save us. People who refuse to be quiet do."

The room rose. The sound buoyed her for a heartbeat. Then it broke into logistics—hands, cameras, promises. Malcolm's presence at her shoulder cut through the noise.

"Car's ready," he murmured.

They exited through a side door into a rain-slick alley. The first car idled, lights dim. Giselle slid in with Eva. Serena stayed back with Malcolm for the second car.

As they pulled away, Giselle angled her phone. "This is Giselle Laurent," she said evenly. "We're en route to a meeting requested by anonymous parties tied to the harassment campaign. We're recording for safety. If you're seeing this later, it means we refused silence."

Eva adjusted the lens to catch street signs. "Steady," she murmured.

The harbor's scent arrived before the water—diesel, salt, rust. The warehouse waited at the end of the street, its roll-up door half open.

The second car pulled in behind them. Malcolm stepped out first, silhouette calm. A figure emerged from the shadows: younger, hoodie up, a white envelope in his hand.

"For you," he said to Giselle. "From a friend."

"Friends sign names," she said.

He smiled, thin. "This one prefers postage."

Malcolm slit the envelope with his key. Inside was a glossy photo. Giselle knew it instantly: her living room, the queen on the sill, turned toward the street.

The caption scrawled beneath: *There are no private stages.*

Heat surged through her, then clarity. She raised her phone, lens catching the photo in Malcolm's hand, the shadowed warehouse behind.

"Thank you," she said, voice steady. "You've just confirmed a felony."

The messenger's smile faltered.

"Tell your employer," she added, "that the play ends with the audience throwing tomatoes."

Malcolm slid the photo back into the envelope. He motioned for the driver. Time to go.

They left smoothly, Eva already uploading the footage to mirrored drives. In the rear window, the dock shrank to shadow.

Her phone buzzed once more. Serena's text: *Tell me you got that on camera.*

Giselle typed back: *Every frame.*

The queen in her pocket felt lighter. Not because the game was over, but because—for the first time—she'd moved first.

Chapter Nineteen

Unmasking

The video leaked before dawn.

Giselle hadn't planned it that way. She'd handed the footage to Eva for safekeeping, encrypted and backed up, intending to control the release. But the internet had its own tempo. At five a.m., hashtags trended with her name. By six, blogs were running stills from the dock—the hooded messenger, the envelope, Malcolm's calm silhouette, and her voice declaring the harassment a felony.

By the time she woke at seven, her phone was vibrating nonstop. Missed calls, new emails, notifications stacked in neon. Serena was the first voice she heard, calling through the noise.

"You're everywhere," Serena said. "CNN, morning radio, three podcasts I didn't even know existed. They're calling you fearless."

Giselle sat up slowly, hair mussed, throat dry. She reached for the chess queen on her nightstand and held it like an anchor. "Fearless is a lie. But I'll take it."

"You've forced their hand," Serena said. "That video is proof, and it's public. No more shadows."

"No," Giselle murmured. "Now the shadows get louder."

She dressed in silence, choosing a navy sheath dress and simple pearls. It was a costume, she knew, but costumes were part of survival. When she arrived at the office, cameras waited on the sidewalk.

Reporters shouted her name, questions flying: *Who are they? Why target you? Are you afraid?*

She smiled, said nothing, and walked inside. Silence could be stronger than any quote.

Her team was buzzing, excitement threaded with nerves. They greeted her like she'd become something larger than their boss, a symbol of resistance wrapped in designer heels. Giselle played the part, but beneath it her pulse thudded. Symbols were brittle. One wrong move, and they shattered.

Malcolm arrived at noon. He didn't push through the front with the press. He slipped in through a service entrance, as steady as always. Giselle found him waiting in her office, hands folded, posture calm.

"You didn't release it," he said.

"No," she answered. "Eva?"

"Not Eva. Someone inside her circle. It doesn't matter. It's out now."

She paced, heels striking the floor. "Then we use it. We pivot. Every question they throw, I turn back on the watchers. They want me to look hunted. I'll look hunted and unbroken."

"They'll escalate," Malcolm warned.

"They already have."

He studied her for a long moment. "You're stronger than I expected."

"You underestimated me?" she asked, arching a brow.

"I hoped for it," he said simply. "Because strength this visible paints targets brighter."

She hated that he was right. She hated more that part of her liked hearing him admit he had hoped she was ordinary.

At three, Eva stormed in with a laptop under her arm, her lipstick fresh and her eyes sharp enough to cut steel.

"You've gone viral," she said. "It's chaos. Some believe you. Some call it performance art. Some already spin conspiracy that you staged it yourself."

"Let them," Giselle said. "Noise is cover. Truth slips sharper in chaos."

Eva placed the laptop on the desk and opened a file. "We traced the suit from the lobby last night. He's tied to a shell corporation registered two weeks ago. A funnel account. It links back to one of the old Harrington firms."

Malcolm's shoulders tightened, the only outward sign of anger. "Elias."

"Or someone using his ruins," Eva said. "Either way, the watchers have financial bones in the dirt you dug up."

Giselle leaned against the desk, arms folded. "So the ghost of your brother funds the people sending me lilies and chess metaphors."

"Yes," Malcolm said quietly.

Eva turned to Giselle. "Do you trust him?"

The question landed heavy. Giselle glanced at Malcolm, saw the steadiness in his face, the calm that could mean loyalty or concealment.

"I trust leverage," she said at last. "And right now, Malcolm has as much to lose as I do."

Eva didn't look satisfied, but she closed the laptop. "Then we push harder. The leak worked. Next, we flood them. Speeches, panels, interviews. The more public you are, the fewer corners they can trap you in."

"Until they change tactics," Malcolm murmured.

"Then we change faster," Giselle said.

That night, Giselle went on live television for the first time in years. The studio lights burned hot, the host's smile sharper than the questions. She answered carefully, weaving narrative like silk: visibility as survival, scrutiny as safety. She spoke of courage without naming herself courageous. By the end, the host looked rattled, the studio audience leaned forward, and Giselle knew she had delivered exactly what the watchers hated most—control.

When she stepped out into the cool night air, flashes popped. Cameras, microphones, shouts. She felt it again, though—the weight of eyes that weren't the press. Watching, not reporting.

Her phone buzzed in her clutch. A message. No photo this time. Just words: *Queens forget pawns bleed first.*

Her stomach tightened. She typed back before she could stop herself: *Touch her and the game ends.*

There was no reply. But across the street, a man in a cap lowered his phone and melted into the crowd.

Giselle stood tall, lifted her chin for the cameras, and walked toward the waiting car. She slid inside, Serena already there, arms folded, expression fierce.

"They won't touch me," Serena said, reading her mind. "I'm not afraid."

Giselle looked at her, at the friend who had walked through every storm at her side. Fear curled sharp in her chest, not for herself but for the cost Serena might pay.

"They should be afraid," Giselle whispered. "Because if they come for you, I burn the board."

The car pulled into traffic, city lights sliding across their faces. Somewhere above, unseen eyes watched. But for the first time, Giselle hoped the watchers were afraid, too.

Chapter Twenty

Firebreak

Sleep came late and left early. Giselle woke to rain needling the windows, the city smudged into grayscale. The headlines still churned her name—clips from the dock, quotes from the interview, think pieces that tried to turn her into metaphor. She let them. Symbols were useful until they weren't.

By eight, she'd built a list across two pages: security upgrades, media hits, donor calls for the nonprofit, routes to swap, decoys to deploy. A campaign wasn't just message; it was logistics. And logistics saved lives.

Serena arrived with croissants, hair in a scarf, eyes bright despite the storm. "You're trending," she said by way of hello. "Half the internet wants to be you. The other half thinks you're a psyop. Congratulations on becoming irresistible content."

"Content pays the bills," Giselle said, taking the bag. "And sometimes buys us time."

They ate at the counter like they used to when rent was a dare, then worked the list: new locks, new cameras, a second phone on a clean plan, a travel router with a hardware kill switch. Serena made calls with cheerful menace; Giselle scheduled interviews with surgical restraint. Visibility without oversaturation—floodlights aimed, not flung.

At ten, Malcolm texted: *Two updates. Docks node dark. New chatter near Midtown financial district. Also—Elias.*

She stared at the name until her jaw ached. *Alive?*

Unknown, came back. *But a lawyer who used to front for him filed an appearance on behalf of an "interested party" in a civil forfeiture case. Shell on shell. It smells like him.*

Her pulse hitched. Elias had been gravity without pity—charming, solvent, then terminally selfish. The watchers might be wearing his corpse like a coat. Or he might be inside it, breathing.

Meet? she typed.

Glass House. Noon. Public, he replied.

Serena watched her tuck the second phone into her bag. "You're going to see him."

"Public," Giselle said. "And short."

"Short is not one of your gifts," Serena muttered, but she kissed two fingers and tapped them against Giselle's shoulder. A blessing dressed as sass. "Text me if anything smells wrong. I'll appear with righteous eyebrows."

Rain thinned to a mist as Giselle crossed the lobby at Glass House. The host clocked her immediately—the dress, the press aura—and ushered her toward the back. Malcolm was already there, a black umbrella drying by his chair, glass of water sweating circles onto the table. His posture read neither victory nor defeat; he collected facts the way other men collected watches.

"Your shadow got louder," he said by way of greeting.

"Which one?"

"The one with my brother's shoes," he answered.

Her stomach tightened. "Is it him?"

"I don't know," he said, and the steadiness of that admission landed like respect. "But someone who benefits from his absence is paying people who know our names." He slid a folder across the table. Inside:

filings, email headers, a flow chart Eva would appreciate—arrows between shell corps, arrows between banks, arrows pointing back to a PO box that physically existed inside a coworking space twelve blocks away.

Giselle touched the page like it might burn. "You want to go now."

"I want to be seen going," he said. "They expect me to hide. We'll do the opposite. Public office hours."

"Daylight is our ally," she murmured, surprised to hear Aunt Alicia in her mouth again.

They left separately and met again as strangers two blocks from the coworking space. The lobby was a curated jungle—fiddle-leaf figs, poured concrete, a neon sign promising GOOD ENERGY. The receptionist wore a hoodie that said it less politely.

"Hi," she chirped. "Do you have a reservation?"

"For a PO box," Giselle said, smile like a blade. She slid a card across the counter—Eva's nonprofit, embossed and official. "We're delivering a records request."

The receptionist hesitated just long enough to confirm guilt, then brightened back to corporate sunlight. "Of course! Second floor."

They took the stairs. On two, white lockers lined a glass corridor. Malcolm checked the number on his printout and stopped at a mailbox whose door was a little too clean. He slid a key he shouldn't have into the slot. It turned like it wanted to be useful.

Inside: a phone. No SIM. A hotel keycard. And a folded note, hand-printed in neat blocks.

Giselle unfolded it. *NO PRIVATE STAGES.* The same hand as the dock envelope. Beneath it, a time and address: *3:00 PM. Gideon Hotel. 14th floor.*

"Bait," Malcolm said.

"Performance," she corrected. "They booked the room and hid the audience."

"Then we change the audience."

They left with the box contents in a courier envelope addressed to Eva. Half a block away, Giselle texted Serena: *Gideon at three. Bring the eyebrows—and the backup plan.* Serena's reply was a photo of a portable floodlight and a grin that could part clouds.

At two forty-five, the Gideon's lobby hummed with the gentle money of midweek meetings. Polished stone, whispering staff, a bar that served confidence in coupe glasses. Giselle and Serena arrived together this time, masks on—sunglasses, impossible calm, laughter for anyone who wanted to read softness into gloss.

Malcolm waited near the elevator bank with a paper bag that turned out to be a motion-activated camera, two adhesive mounts, and a roll of gaffer tape. "If they jam phone signals," he said, "they won't jam physics."

They rode to fourteen with a man in a suit checking three phones, and a woman in gym clothes pretending not to notice she was on the wrong elevator. When the doors opened, Giselle walked like she belonged there and Malcolm walked like the hallway owed him rent. Serena walked like intimidation in sneakers.

Room 1407 opened on the first try. Inside, neutral beauty: beige sofa, art that looked expensive and meant nothing, curtains heavy enough to convince the eye it was always evening. On the coffee table waited another white envelope beside a plate of hotel fruit.

"Do not eat the metaphor," Serena said, side-eying the grapes.

Malcolm mounted the first camera high on the bookshelf and the second in the corner lamp's shade. Giselle scanned outlets, vents, the baseboards' meet-cutes with the carpet. She found one mic in the smoke detector, two more in the curtain valance, and a device under the sofa that looked like a charger and wasn't. She held each up. "Amateurs."

"Amateurs with budget," Malcolm said. He checked his watch. "Three o'clock."

Giselle opened the envelope. A single glossy photo slid out—this time not of her, but of Malcolm ten years younger, standing on courthouse steps beside a woman whose lipstick could cut glass. Eva Sloane, mid-sentence, fury in the angle of her hand. On the back, more block letters: *SOME PAWNS PROMOTE THEMSELVES.*

Serena hissed. "They want you to doubt each other."

"Or they want us to reenact an old scene badly," Giselle said. She flipped the photo face down. "No curtain call."

The door handle clicked.

Serena disappeared behind the bathroom door, phone in one hand, floodlight in the other. Malcolm stepped to the side of the entry, shadow quiet. Giselle stayed visible—queen in her pocket, chin high.

A man entered in a raincoat that had never seen a storm. He was the kind of mid-forties handsome money buys with a gym membership: healthy, bland, forgettable by design. He shut the door with the deliberation of someone who liked the sound of locks. When he smiled, it didn't reach his eyes.

"Ms. Laurent," he said, as if they were co-hosts. "Thank you for coming."

"I didn't," she said. "I arrived."

His smile twitched. He glanced at Malcolm and elected not to speak to him. "We can help each other," he said to Giselle instead. "Visibility is a double-edged sword. You're bleeding. I'm offering a bandage."

"Name," she said.

"Call me Preston," he said too easily.

"Real name," she said.

He ignored the prompt. "You're interfering with recoveries that belong to people more patient than the law. Step back, and the temperature drops. Keep dancing in the lights, and—" He spread his hands. "Accidents."

"Accidents like flowers," Serena said, stepping from the bathroom as the floodlight fired to life, washing the room in unflattering truth. Preston flinched and blinked at the sudden glare.

Giselle smiled with all her teeth. "Smile for the cheap cameras."

He recovered quickly. "Recording won't help you. We own erasure."

"Try erasing light," Serena said, angling the beam.

Preston's gaze slid to Malcolm with bored contempt. "You always did trade one woman's safety for another's silence."

"Interesting," Giselle said, before old poison could bloom. "You rehearsed the wrong monologue."

Preston's smile thinned. "A queen who thinks she's a playwright." He reached into his coat—not fast, not a weapon, something equally ugly: a paper with letterhead. "Subpoena," he announced. "From a court that still prefers its files unbothered." He placed it on the table like a curse. "Turn over all materials related to the dock incident. Or be held in contempt."

Giselle didn't touch the paper. "Is contempt bailable?"

Preston blinked. "Excuse me?"

"It would be my pleasure," she said. "Public records love a good contempt story."

He watched her, calculation stuttering. "You think you can win by embarrassing people."

"I think you confuse shame with strategy," she said. "And both with power." She nodded toward the envelope he'd failed to notice—the one from the coworking box, already scanned and sent to Eva. "You wanted private stages. We sell tickets."

Preston exhaled through his nose, anger tight but practiced. "Last offer. Step back. The queen sleeps. Your pawn stays unbloodied."

Serena's voice lost its humor. "Say my name if you're going to threaten me."

Preston didn't. Cowards rarely did. He checked the door like a man who preferred exits to answers. "We're finished."

"Not yet," Malcolm said, finally speaking. "Tell Elias Harrington I recognize his handwriting."

The first true crack slid through Preston's expression. "You're chasing ghosts," he snapped. "Ghosts don't bleed."

"No," Malcolm said softly. "Men do."

Preston left with the practiced economy of a messenger who believed his message self-authenticating. The door clicked. Silence expanded, then snapped under Serena's breath.

"Did he just subpoena our audacity?"

Giselle picked up the paper with two fingers and smiled without warmth. "He tried to subpoena our fear." She turned it for Malcolm to see. The clerk's stamp was real; the case number was a shell; the signature belonged to a judge who had retired last year. "Forgery with a budget."

Serena killed the floodlight; the cheap cameras blinked their own conclusions. Malcolm peeled the bug from the smoke detector and dropped it into the ice bucket, where it clicked like a cicada and died.

Giselle set the forged subpoena beside the face-down photo and the envelope. Three props for a scene that would not play the way they'd planned. She could already feel the shape of the next act: public, louder, riskier—and safer in its own paradoxical way.

Her phone buzzed. Eva: *Got your package. Working the case number. Also: a tip—anonymous—says "E" will call tonight. Unknown whether Elias or echo. Keep a recorder near your landline.*

"Landline?" Serena said, peering over her shoulder. "What is this, 2003?"

"An antique with fewer apps," Giselle murmured. She pocketed the forged paper and the photo. "Let's give the past a dial tone."

Back on the street, rain had returned with purpose. People hurried with heads down, the city's heartbeat damp but insistent. As they split—Serena to stage the press angle, Malcolm to brief Eva, Giselle to prepare for a call that might finally have a voice—the queen in Giselle's pocket nudged her hip, a reminder and a dare.

She touched it once, like a talisman. Firebreaks, she thought—the line you burn on purpose so the rest doesn't. She could feel the flames trying to run ahead of her. She would set her own line first.

At home, she placed the recorder by the old landline she kept for nostalgia and outages. The rain scratched at the windows like hungry code. She changed into soft clothes that didn't creak when she breathed and tied her hair back, a soldier's braid for the living room. At 8:59, the phone rang. One long tone, like a held note.

Giselle lifted the receiver, steady. "This is Giselle."

A breath. Then a voice she'd never heard and almost recognized.

"Little brother always did love a stage," the man said. "Shall we step into the wings?"

Chapter Twenty-One

The Voice

The receiver felt heavier than it should. Giselle pressed it to her ear, heart thudding steady but hard, the queen warm in her pocket like a coal. The voice on the other end was low, unhurried, textured with age and theater.

"Who is this?" she asked, though she already knew the only answer that mattered.

"Names are costumes," the man said. "And you've always been good with costumes. Call me what he did. Call me Elias."

The syllables sank into her chest like cold water. She swallowed once. "You're supposed to be gone."

"Gone is relative," Elias said. "Some disappear to punish. Some disappear to live. I chose the second. I see now my little brother prefers the first."

"You've been watching me."

"You're difficult not to watch," Elias replied. "The woman who stole his rhythm and rewrote it into her own. You've made yourself central, Giselle. Queens don't stay offstage."

Her mouth tightened. "Why me?"

"You're leverage. You're narrative. You're beauty on the board where Malcolm has only weight. The people who pay to keep me breathing—they love the shape of you. And they love more that you don't break."

"I'm not here to entertain your patrons," she said coldly.

"You've been entertaining them for weeks," Elias countered. "Every speech, every glare, every denial. They study you the way gamblers study dice. But dice don't talk back."

Her grip on the receiver tightened. "What do you want?"

"To remind you," Elias said softly, "that survival is choreography. And choreography always has a director. You've mistaken yourself for one."

Giselle exhaled, steady. "And you think it's you."

"It is me," Elias said. "Always has been. Malcolm dances because I build the stage. You—" His voice shifted, almost warm. "You could be more than a queen. You could be the whole game."

She laughed sharply. "And what, kneel at the edge of your stage until you decide I'm worth moving?"

"No," he said. "Stand beside me. Imagine it: you with your lights, me with my shadows. Together, no one touches us. You'd never be hunted again."

The temptation, spoken so calmly, almost disguised itself as protection. For half a breath, she imagined it—her face on screens, his reach in every ledger, the watchers defanged because they were no longer outside the circle but inside, chained to her rules.

Then she remembered Serena's laugh, Malcolm's steady silences, Eva's relentless clarity. She remembered the lily in a florist's box, the queen slid under her door, the envelope that had turned her home into theatre.

"You mistake me," she said evenly. "I don't want to be untouchable. I want to be unowned."

The silence that followed was sharp as broken glass.

"You sound like him," Elias said at last, the warmth gone. "Defiant, righteous. He'll get you killed. And when you break, it won't be because of me—it will be because of your loyalty to people who mistake affection for armor."

"You're afraid," she said quietly.

Another pause. Then a chuckle, soft but tight. "I'm patient. Queens die slower than pawns. Goodnight, Giselle."

The line clicked dead.

She set the receiver down carefully, though her hand shook. For a long moment, she sat at the kitchen counter, rain thrumming against the glass, the recorder's light blinking to confirm every word had been captured. Proof, Eva would say. Evidence, Malcolm would call it. To Giselle, it felt like prophecy.

At nine-thirty, Serena arrived, damp from the storm. She took one look at Giselle's face and set her umbrella aside. "He called."

"Yes."

"Elias."

"Yes."

Serena swore softly, then sat beside her. "And?"

"He wants me beside him. His lights and shadows. His partner."

Serena's eyes narrowed. "And you told him—"

"That I'm not for sale."

Serena leaned back, tension loosening just a fraction. "Good. Because I was about to stage an intervention with kitchen knives."

Despite herself, Giselle almost smiled.

At ten, Malcolm arrived. He didn't knock, didn't wait. He came in like someone with less time than truth. "He called."

"Yes," Giselle said.

"I heard the recording."

Her eyes widened. "How?"

"Eva routed the line," he said. "We needed confirmation."

"You're surveilling me."

"I'm protecting you," he corrected.

The distinction burned. "That's the same argument he made."

Malcolm's face didn't change, but his shoulders stiffened. "And what did you answer him?"

"That I don't kneel," she said.

For the first time, something like pride flickered in his eyes. "Then he'll move faster now. Elias never forgives rejection."

Serena crossed her arms. "Neither do I, but I don't send lilies with condolence notes."

Malcolm ignored her. "We need to tighten circles. Fewer contacts. No unplanned appearances. They'll come harder, louder. And Elias will make it personal."

"It already is," Giselle said.

"Yes," Malcolm admitted. "But now it's worse. He's turned you into his audience. And Elias never performs without blood."

Giselle rose, crossing to the window. The city glittered wet and merciless. Her reflection looked back at her, perfect and tired. She pressed her fingers against the glass, the queen heavy in her pocket.

"They've been playing games," she said. "Pieces on boards, flowers in boxes. But this—" She turned to face them. "This is a war declaration."

Neither argued. The rain thickened outside, streaking the glass like ink. Giselle stood tall, steady, the weight of Elias's voice still in her chest, her own words louder now.

She would not kneel. She would not break. And she would not, under any stage light or shadow, let Elias Harrington write her ending.

Chapter Twenty-Two

Breaking Point

By morning, the storm had passed, but the city didn't look cleansed. It looked raw, scraped down to concrete and noise. Giselle stood at her window, coffee in hand, watching people hurry through puddles. Ordinary lives continuing, as if hers hadn't tilted toward something dangerous enough to warp the air.

Her phone buzzed with notifications: interviews requests, hashtags, panel invites. She ignored them all. After Elias's call, visibility no longer felt like safety. It felt like bait.

At ten, Eva arrived without warning. She didn't waste time on pleasantries. She dropped her tote on the table and opened her laptop. "The call was logged, traced, scrubbed. No fingerprints. But the audio is clean. His voice is his signature."

"I thought Elias was a ghost," Giselle said.

Eva's lipstick curved in something like disdain. "Ghosts don't leave subpoenas on hotel tables."

Malcolm joined them minutes later, his presence quiet as always. He sat, folded his hands, and looked at Giselle. "He'll escalate now."

"He already has," she replied. "The moment he said my name, escalation became air."

Serena arrived last, carrying pastries she barely touched. She slouched into a chair and watched the three of them with narrowed eyes. "So what's the plan? Because sitting here naming him like Voldemort isn't going to keep us alive."

Eva's fingers danced across the keyboard. "He has nodes—finance, muscle, optics. We can't collapse all three at once. But we can target a weak one. Hit it loud. Force him to react."

"Which one?" Giselle asked.

"Optics," Eva said. "The people who launder his story into something respectable. You wound narrative, you wound power."

Serena smirked. "That's Giselle's specialty."

Giselle's pulse steadied. "So we turn his tactics on him. Plant doubt in the shadows. Expose whispers before they calcify into threats."

Malcolm shook his head. "Elias thrives on doubt. He'll spin suspicion into loyalty. If you show cracks, he feeds on them."

Eva's gaze sharpened. "Not if we choose the crack."

They argued the details for hours, voices low but taut, the air thick with tension. Finally, they agreed: they would stage a reveal at Friday's press conference, a controlled leak that tied Elias to the forged subpoena and the shell corporations. It wouldn't dismantle him, but it would mark him.

Marking Elias Harrington was like drawing blood in shark water. But sometimes blood was necessary to redirect the frenzy.

That evening, Giselle prepared herself. She dressed for cameras even in her living room, rehearsed lines until they felt like truth. But beneath the polish, her hands trembled.

Serena noticed. "You don't have to do this."

"I do," Giselle said. "Because if I don't, he wins without even showing up."

At midnight, unable to sleep, she wandered her loft. The queen sat on the sill, facing the street. She picked it up, rolled it in her palm, then set it back with deliberate force. "Not yours," she whispered to Elias, wherever he was.

The phone rang once. The landline again. She froze, staring at it. The recorder was ready, but her heart wasn't.

She lifted the receiver.

No voice. Just silence.

Then breathing. Slow, patient, familiar.

"Say it," she whispered.

The line clicked dead.

Her body trembled, fury overtaking fear. She slammed the phone down and leaned against the counter, chest heaving. They weren't just watching—they were listening for weakness. Testing her silence.

The next morning, Giselle walked into the office early. She gathered her team, smiling with the same flawless ease as always, and assigned tasks for the press conference. No one noticed the new sharpness in her tone, the edge beneath the polish. She was done waiting for cues from Elias. She would set her own stage, her own tempo.

By noon, Malcolm texted her: *You ready?*

She replied: *More than ready. I'm furious.*

He responded with a single word. *Good.*

The press conference was scheduled for Friday. That gave them two days to sharpen their knives, polish their story, and dare Elias to come into the light.

But on Wednesday night, as Giselle walked home alone after a strategy session, a black sedan slowed beside her. The window rolled down just far enough for a hand to appear. A lily dropped onto the wet pavement.

The car sped off, taillights bleeding into the dark.

Giselle stood frozen for a moment, staring at the flower gleaming white under the streetlight. Her stomach twisted. She crouched, picked it up, and snapped the stem clean in two.

When she looked up, a camera lens glinted from a rooftop. Watching, always watching.

She lifted the broken lily high, let the pieces fall onto the street, and walked away without looking back.

They wanted performance. She would give them one. But it would be her script, not theirs.

Chapter Twenty-Three

Prebunk

Thursday arrived brittle and bright, the kind of hard light that flattened texture and made everything look truer than it wanted to be. Giselle woke before her alarm and lay listening to the city shiver itself awake. She replayed the lily breaking in her hands the night before, the clean snap that felt like a vow. They wanted symbols; she would decide what they meant.

By eight, she was in motion. Coffee scalding, hair pulled into a sleek knot, blazer the color of resolve. She sent Serena a message—*Nine at the office. We prebunk.*—and shot a separate text to Malcolm and Eva with a single word: *Today.*

Serena arrived in sneakers and a trench that looked like it could win an argument. She tossed her bag on the couch and arched a brow. "Prebunk?"

"Not debunk," Giselle said, pacing. "Debunk chases lies. Prebunk plants architecture so the lies have nowhere to land. Before Elias pushes a smear, we salt the earth."

Eva joined by video from a quiet room with a corkboard behind her that looked like a conspiracy theorist's dream and a prosecutor's pride. "What's our threat model?"

Giselle ticked them off with manicured fingers. "One: doctored video—me and Malcolm in a compromised scene. Two: invented texts that show I'm coordinating blackmail. Three: a financial 'leak' that frames our nonprofit contract as money laundering."

Serena whistled softly. "I hate that all those feel obvious."

"Good," Giselle said. "Obvious is predictable. We can build guardrails."

Eva's mouth tilted, not quite a smile. "What do you propose?"

"Three moves," Giselle said. "First, we publish raw assets now—behind-the-scenes footage, full-context clips from the dock, our hotel meeting from two angles. No edits. Date-stamped. If they try to slice, we show the loaf."

"Second," Serena cut in, catching the rhythm, "we pre-register a sworn affidavit with timestamps from last night and this morning. I'll sign too. If a deepfake drops, we can point to contemporaneous records."

"Third," Giselle said, "we announce an independent forensic review with a firm that scares judges and tech bros equally. We invite them publicly, on the record, and we share the chain of custody. If Elias tries to dump false files, we make accepting them a confession."

Eva sat back, considering. "Aggressive. Good. I can add a fourth: I'll leak to a friendly that an unnamed source warned us about a coordinated disinformation push. They'll publish a piece at noon explaining prebunking as a concept. It inoculates casual onlookers. And it annoys him."

Giselle felt the click she always felt when language snapped into place. "We salt the earth," she repeated. "Then we plant our field."

By ten, the machine spun. Serena wrangled release forms and uploaded full-length clips to a secure public archive with links that couldn't be quietly edited. Eva drafted the leak and messaged her journalist with the kind of restraint that sold urgency. Giselle recorded a two-minute statement in a white-walled conference room, no makeup correction, no soft light, only a clean frame and a steady voice.

"Here is the truth before the lies," she said to the camera. "We expect a coordinated attempt to misrepresent what we've recorded and who we are. So we're sharing the receipts up front. If you see a clip without the link to full context, assume someone prefers you ignorant. We don't."

She finished, exhaled, and sent it live on the nonprofit's channel and her own. Within minutes, comments stacked, some supportive, some suspicious, most hooked. Attention was a river; she had just placed stones in its course.

At noon, the prebunk article hit. The headline was clean and brutal: *Before You Watch the Next Viral Clip, Consider Who Cut It.* The piece quoted security researchers and described deepfakes like counterfeit bills—convincing until the bank touches them. It mentioned Giselle's campaign without making her the entire case study. Perfect. She forwarded it to Malcolm with a single word: *Armor.*

He replied: *Frontline at three. Dock cluster flickered again. Might be noise, might be nerve.*

She stared at the message. *Frontline?*

Where we stand when they charge.

Serena leaned in the doorway, reading her face the way only Serena could. "He's going hunting."

"We all are," Giselle said. "But in daylight."

By two, the counteroffensive arrived on schedule. A burner account posted a grainy video of Giselle entering a hotel room with a man in a raincoat. The angle favored innuendo. The caption slithered: *Queen's nights aren't so clean.* Within five minutes, three more accounts posted identical copies, like a choir that didn't bother to harmonize.

Serena rolled her eyes. "They always choose the laziest adjectives."

Giselle didn't blink. She dropped the link to the full Gideon footage in the replies, pinning the timecodes where Preston delivered the forged subpoena and threatened Serena. The countered narrative spread fast. The cheap posts kept coming—text screenshots with formatting errors, a PDF pretending to be a bank transfer with the decimal in the wrong place—but the prebunk had already placed doubt where they needed certainty. The comments turned skeptical. The choir lost its sheet music.

At three, Malcolm texted: *Meet me. Corner of Bracken and 9th. Two blocks north of the coworking building.*

Serena laced up her sneakers like armor. "We go together."

Giselle hesitated, then nodded. "Eva, patch into our phones."

"Already there," Eva said. "If they jam, I'll lose you. Otherwise, I'm your ghost."

The corner of Bracken and 9th smelled like rain drying on hot brick. Delivery trucks grumbled, a food cart hissed onion and fat, and a man in a yellow poncho sold knockoff umbrellas to a sky that had stopped crying. Malcolm stood half in shadow, the city's noise skimming past him like he was a rock in a stream.

"Your prebunk worked," he said as they approached. "They'll adapt."

"They always do," Giselle answered. "What do you have?"

He handed her a single-page printout. A schedule. Room bookings at the Gideon. The PO box locker access times. A pattern that spelled out arrogance: the same card used for both, the same ten-minute window before and after each "meeting" to plant, retrieve, edit.

"They're running a playbook," Serena said, tapping the paper. "Same slots, same routes. Men love routines they can mistake for control."

"Look at the next reservation," Malcolm said, pointing to a line two hours from now. "Room 1411. Three-thirty to four fifteen. 'Private wellness consult.'"

Giselle felt the lift of adrenaline like a small airplane catching a pocket of air. "They expect us to be too busy cleaning myths to show up for reality."

"We show up," Serena said. "With friends."

They moved fast. Eva dispatched two trusted volunteers with body cams and a lawyer whose superpower was smiling like a warning. Giselle called the Gideon's manager from the nonprofit line and booked the room next door—1413—for a "donor thank-you call." Serena texted three reporters she knew could keep their heads when the air smelled like blood.

At three twenty-seven, they rode the elevator together. Giselle felt calm settle over her like a shawl. Serena checked the floodlight battery and winked. Malcolm said nothing, but his presence filled the space between them. The doors slid open to fourteen and the hallway smelled like lemon and nerve.

They entered 1413 and set their stage: cameras angled, mics hot, the connecting door inspected and found unlocked because hotels rarely believed people were interesting. Through the adjoining seam, voices murmured—too precise to be guests, too careless to be professionals. A man laughed. Another quieted him. Papers rustled. Plastic peeled. Tape stretched.

Giselle held up three fingers. Two. One.

Serena opened the connecting door with the casual grace of a woman pushing into a brunch reservation and flipped on the floodlight. Light smashed the shadows. Four men froze mid-scene: one with a camera rig, one holding a folder, one placing a bug under the table, one turning toward a bathroom where a fifth voice cursed and fell silent.

"Hi," Serena said sweetly. "Welcome to the end of your private wellness."

The lawyer stepped in, badge on a lanyard, voice calm. "You're being recorded. Please do not destroy evidence."

One of the men bolted for the hall. Malcolm caught the door without touching him, just standing where the exit needed him to move. The runner decided against it. He set the bug down like it had grown teeth.

Giselle stepped forward, queen in her pocket, fury in her spine. She didn't shout. She didn't need to. "You'll tell us who sent you," she said evenly. "Or you'll tell the district attorney when this plays on every feed that pays attention."

The folder man smirked. "You think the DA cares?"

Eva's voice came through Giselle's earpiece, dry and delighted. "He will in three, two, one—"

The hallway filled with footsteps and authority. Building security, two uniformed officers, a plainclothes detective with a face like a closed door. The reporters Serena had texted stood politely behind them, eyes bright, phones lowered until permission went up. It did, quickly. The law liked cameras lately; cameras liked the law back.

The men blustered, pointed, lied poorly. The bug under the table looked like guilt with a sticker. The camera rig looked like a confession with a lens. The folder contained copies of the forged subpoena with fresher ink and a cover letter from another shell with a name Eva would break by dinner.

The detective read the top page, glanced at Malcolm, then at Giselle. His tone held no sympathy, only agenda. "You want to make a statement?"

Giselle nodded once. "On the record."

They gave it, clear and surgical. No grandstanding, no trembling. Serena added a line about lilies. Malcolm said Elias's name without flinching. The detective didn't react. The reporters kept their faces blank, their pencils hungry. The men in the room looked smaller in daylight than they had in the dark.

It took an hour to process. An hour to bag the devices, log the chain of custody, receive a copy of the incident report that would be redactable later and undeniable now. When it was done, the detective handed Giselle a card. "If 'E' calls again, let him know we listen too."

Back on the street, the sky had softened. Traffic hummed. A dog barked at a pigeon and lost. Serena whooped once, a short victorious sound. Malcolm looked at Giselle, something like relief ghosting the edge of his composure.

"You prebunked," he said. "Then you broke their scene."

"They built a set," she said. "We turned on the lights."

Her phone buzzed. A new message, unknown number. A photo of the hotel door: 1413. Caption: *Cute.*

Giselle typed back: *True. Friday will be beautiful.*

No answer. Just the city, moving around them, as if it had always planned to, as if this had always been the way forward: not away from danger, but through it, with the truth taped down and the lights impossible to dim.

Chapter Twenty-Four

Fault Lines in Daylight

Friday dawned sharp and restless. The air held that brittle kind of calm that always broke into storms later. Giselle dressed as if the press conference were a battlefield—navy suit, hair sculpted, pearls precise as punctuation. Serena teased her for looking like a senator's nightmare, but her voice was taut with nerves.

They drove together, windows tinted, the queen tucked into Giselle's jacket pocket. Cameras waited outside the venue already, clustered like birds sensing a change in weather. Reporters shouted questions as she stepped into the lobby: *Who's Elias Harrington? Is he alive? Did you orchestrate the leak?* She gave them nothing but a smile sharp enough to wound.

Inside, the stage was set. Rows of chairs, a podium with microphones fanned like metal flowers, a projection screen behind her flashing the nonprofit's logo in looping calm. Eva stood off to the side, phone in hand, eyes scanning constantly. Malcolm leaned against a pillar, the picture of composed tension. His presence calmed her in a way she hated admitting.

At ten sharp, the lights dimmed and the press hushed. Giselle walked to the podium, every heel strike deliberate, her pulse a drumbeat in her ears. She didn't bother with introductions.

"You've heard rumors," she began, voice steady. "You've seen clips, screenshots, fragments that pretend to be truth. We expected this. We told you to expect this. And now, as promised, we share the receipts."

The screen lit up with full-length footage from the Gideon—unedited, timestamped, dual angles. Preston's raincoat, his forged subpoena, Serena's floodlight burning the pretense away. Gasps moved through the room like wind.

Giselle didn't pause. "Here are the filings that show shell corporations tied to familiar names. Here is the chain of custody for evidence handed over two days ago. Here is the sworn affidavit from myself and Serena, timestamped before the smears began. We are not hiding. We are not running. And we are not afraid."

The questions came fast, shouted over each other: *Who funds him? Why target you? Do you believe Elias Harrington is alive?*

Giselle raised a hand, silencing the room. "What I believe is this: secrecy empowers predators. Visibility disarms them. Whether Elias Harrington is alive, or whether someone uses his name as a mask, is irrelevant. What matters is this—he and his allies want you to question your own eyes. I will not allow that. And neither should you."

The room erupted again. Cameras clicked like gunfire. Eva gestured, signaling she'd push the files to multiple outlets immediately. Malcolm stayed still, unreadable, but his gaze never left Giselle's face.

When she stepped down, Serena caught her arm. "You just declared war in high definition."

"Good," Giselle said. "Now let him answer in daylight."

But daylight had its own cracks. As they moved toward the exit, her phone buzzed. Unknown number. She opened it without slowing. A photo filled the screen: Malcolm at sixteen, standing beside Elias on a courthouse step. Elias's arm draped around his younger brother's shoulders, his smile both pride and ownership.

The caption: *Loyalty fractures louder than lies.*

She stopped walking. The world seemed to hush around her, the photo burning into her vision. Serena glanced down at the screen and hissed. "They're trying to pit you."

Malcolm leaned close, eyes flicking to the phone, then to her. His voice was steady, almost soft. "It's bait."

But the doubt threaded in her stomach anyway. The resemblance between then and now, the shadow of history she hadn't touched. She pocketed the phone, mask sliding back into place. "We'll talk later."

They made it to the car. Eva joined them in the backseat, already typing furiously. "Coverage is everywhere. Half the outlets run the files as evidence. The other half question your timing. But they all lead with your face."

"And Elias?" Giselle asked.

"Quiet," Eva said. "Which means he's furious."

The car moved through the city, but Giselle barely saw the streets. The photo replayed in her head, Elias's hand on Malcolm's shoulder, the caption digging in like a splinter. She wanted to believe Malcolm's steadiness, his loyalty, his silence that had always felt like shelter. But Elias's voice echoed: *Queens forget pawns bleed first.*

At her loft, Serena insisted on staying the night. Malcolm lingered too, silent as furniture, though his eyes never stopped scanning. Eva left with promises to monitor chatter.

By midnight, the loft was quiet but charged. Serena slept on the couch, one arm draped across her eyes. Giselle stood at the window, queen in her palm, staring out at the city's restless lights. Malcolm joined her, silent for a long moment before he spoke.

"You saw the photo."

"Yes."

"You doubt me."

She didn't answer.

His jaw tightened. "He raised me for a while. He funded me. He used me. But I am not him. You need to know that."

Her grip on the queen was tight enough to leave marks. "Do I?"

"Yes," he said, voice low but firm. "Because if you don't, this ends here. Not with Elias winning, but with us breaking ourselves for him."

She turned, met his eyes. For the first time, she saw not just steadiness but desperation, the raw edge beneath composure. He wasn't asking for faith. He was demanding it.

Serena stirred, mumbling in her sleep. Giselle looked away, the queen heavy in her palm. She slipped it into her pocket and walked back toward the kitchen.

"I'll decide what I believe in the morning," she said.

Malcolm didn't follow.

The rain started again, soft at first, then hard enough to drown the silence.

Chapter Twenty-Five

Splinter

Giselle didn't sleep. The rain's drumming carried her through the night, her mind replaying the photo of Malcolm and Elias again and again, as if the pixels themselves could confess something she missed. By dawn, the city was gray and dripping, the loft silent except for Serena's steady breathing from the couch.

She brewed coffee, but it tasted like ash. When Malcolm emerged from the guest room, his shirt half-buttoned, his expression unreadable, she handed him a mug without meeting his eyes.

"Morning," he said.

Her reply was flat. "Is it?"

He studied her for a beat, then sipped. "You're angry."

"I'm calculating," she corrected. "Anger's easy. Calculation keeps me alive."

Serena stirred, hair wild, voice groggy. "What are we calculating this early?"

"Trust," Giselle said.

The word cracked the air. Serena sat up, blinking between them. "You two need to have this fight without me as the referee."

Malcolm's jaw worked. "I've never lied to you."

"You've never told me everything either," Giselle said. "That's a kind of lie."

"I kept you alive," he countered.

"And Elias thinks he raised you," she shot back. "So tell me, Malcolm—how do I know which brother I'm standing beside?"

The silence after was long, dangerous. Serena broke it with a sharp clap of her hands. "Okay, timeout. We don't implode in pajamas. We get dressed, eat food, and if you're going to accuse each other of being traitors, at least do it after I've brushed my teeth."

Her levity cracked the tension just enough. Giselle turned away, pouring more coffee she wouldn't drink. Malcolm set his mug down and left for the balcony, rain misting his shoulders.

By midmorning, Eva arrived with updates. She placed a folder on the table, her nails clicking against the cardboard. "Coverage is fracturing. Half the city thinks you're crusaders. The other half thinks you're actors in a play Elias directs. And the courts? They're suddenly interested in that forged subpoena. Which means he's nervous."

"Good," Giselle said.

Eva looked at Malcolm, then back at Giselle. "But there's chatter that his next move won't be in filings or flowers. It'll be personal. A spectacle."

"Where?" Serena asked.

Eva hesitated. "Tonight. Union Square. A vigil for financial abuse survivors. Someone leaked that Giselle might attend. If you go, you'll be the centerpiece. If you don't, the absence will be louder."

Giselle leaned back, considering. "He wants me in public. Wants to test whether fear shrinks me."

"Then don't go," Malcolm said instantly.

"No," Giselle replied. "I have to."

Serena groaned. "Of course you do."

Eva tapped the folder. "Then we set conditions. Visible security. Pre-cleared press. And you don't walk anywhere alone."

"Fine," Giselle said.

But the photo still lived under her ribs, Elias's hand on Malcolm's shoulder. The splinter of doubt pulsed every time Malcolm spoke.

That evening, Union Square hummed with soft lights and murmured prayers. Candles dotted the steps, faces turned upward, stories read aloud by survivors who refused to whisper anymore. Giselle stood near the center, Serena on one side, Malcolm on the other, Eva orbiting like a general in the field.

When it was her turn, Giselle stepped forward. The candles flickered, catching her face. She spoke of silence as violence, of shame as architecture, of stories as weapons. She didn't name Elias. She didn't have to. His shadow stretched across every sentence.

The crowd applauded softly, respectfully. Then it shifted—rippling, murmuring—as a figure stepped onto the far side of the steps.

A man in a gray coat, hood up, holding a single chess piece between two fingers.

A queen.

Gasps moved through the crowd. Cameras lifted. Giselle's pulse thundered, but she didn't move.

Serena swore under her breath. Malcolm's hand hovered near hers— not touching, waiting.

The man lifted the queen, then placed it gently on the stone ledge beside a candle. He turned, hood slipping back just enough for the cameras to catch his profile. Strong jaw. Familiar nose. Enough resemblance to ignite whispers.

"Elias," someone murmured.

The man disappeared into the crowd before anyone could stop him.

Chaos erupted—reporters shouting, people pressing forward, security straining. Eva barked orders into her phone. Serena grabbed Giselle's arm. Malcolm stood frozen for a split second, his face pale under the lights.

Back in the car, the city howled around them. Eva replayed footage on her phone. "It's grainy. Deliberate. Enough to suggest without proving. Perfect theater."

Serena shook her head. "He staged a resurrection."

Giselle's chest tightened. "And he chose my stage to do it."

Malcolm spoke for the first time since. His voice was low, raw. "It wasn't him."

Giselle turned sharply. "You sound certain."

"I know his walk," Malcolm said. "I know his shoulders. That wasn't Elias."

"But you knew him," she pressed.

"Yes," he admitted. "Which means I know when a ghost isn't real. But the problem is—" He glanced at her, at Serena, at Eva. "Elias doesn't need to be alive for them to believe he is. Belief is enough."

Silence fell heavy. The city outside their windows blurred into neon and stormlight.

Giselle closed her eyes, the queen's image still glowing behind her lids. Splintering trust, splintering truth. Elias, alive or not, was pulling them apart piece by piece.

And if she didn't choose her next move carefully, the board would collapse before she ever reached the endgame.

Chapter Twenty-Six

The False Resurrection

The car dropped them at Giselle's building just before midnight. The vigil's candlelight still seemed to cling to her coat, cloying in its sweetness, as if wax and smoke had followed her home. She stepped out into the quiet street with Malcolm shadowing her, Serena trailing with her usual commentary, and Eva already typing on her phone as though typing itself were a kind of weapon.

Inside, the loft felt staged—too neat, too carefully arranged, as if someone had anticipated their return. The queen still sat on the sill, angled toward the city like an eye that never blinked. Giselle set her purse down, glanced at it once, and then deliberately looked away.

Serena tossed her keys onto the counter. "We need a rule," she said, voice sharp to hide the tremor beneath it. "If a ghost appears in public, we do not chase it. No candlelight chases. No running after hoods in the rain. No Scooby-Doo."

Eva was already bent over her laptop, cables and files spreading across the island. She didn't look up. "I'm not chasing," she said. "I'm measuring."

Malcolm stood at the window, hands buried deep in his pockets. The reflection made him look older, like a man who had already fought too many wars and found no medals at the end.

Giselle placed the queen on the counter, its ivory weight like a punctuation mark. "Measure fast," she said. "By morning, they'll swear I invited him."

Eva dragged the footage from Union Square frame by frame, her eyes flicking across the screen. "Look here," she murmured. "Knee gait. See the slight drag on the left? Elias broke that ankle in his twenties. Surgery corrected it. This isn't his walk."

Malcolm exhaled slowly, as though something he had been holding for years finally released. "I told you," he said quietly.

Giselle didn't meet his eyes. "A decoy convinces those who want to be convinced," she said. "That's all he needs."

"Height about six foot," Eva continued. "Nose profile similar but not quite right—narrower bridge. Hands younger. They cast him well enough for a crowd, but not for a close-up."

Serena muttered, "Broadway casting on a budget." She rubbed her face. "I hate men who think theater makes them prophets."

A new text buzzed on Giselle's phone. Unknown number. The screen filled with a close-cropped photo of the vigil: the queen perched on the ledge, candlelight glowing around it like an unholy halo. The caption read: *Queens burn prettiest.*

Giselle handed the phone to Eva without comment. Eva snapped a shot of the message, filed it to the secure archive, and kept scrolling. "We flip this tomorrow," she said. "Release gait analysis, call in a podcaster who can explain fakes to the public. If the resurrection collapses in a week, the myth looks cheap."

"A week is long on this board," Giselle replied. "We need hours."

Serena tied her hair back like armor. "Then we give them lightning. Tomorrow, survivors speak—not about you, but with you. If he shows, he's reduced to a heckler."

Eva nodded. "That draws him into a frame he can't control."

Malcolm turned from the window. "He won't come again so soon."

"Then his people will," Giselle said. "And we'll be ready."

Silence fell, heavy but competent. They were tired, but the room felt like strategy had become oxygen.

By two a.m., the plan was sketched. Eva would deliver the gait analysis to two trusted outlets before dawn. Serena would confirm three survivor testimonies for the evening. Malcolm would run the perimeter again, checking locks, cameras, the elevator landing. Giselle showered until the water ran cold, then reemerged to find Serena curled on the couch, Eva still at the keyboard, Malcolm leaning against the window frame like a statue guarding the city.

The landline rang once. Stopped.

Everyone froze.

It rang again.

Giselle picked up, holding the receiver with steady fingers though her stomach flipped.

Breathing. Male. Familiar now.

"Theatrics tonight," the voice drawled.

"Cheap ones," she answered.

"But effective. Half the city believes. Half is enough."

"You sent a boy in your coat," she said. "Was it rental?"

"My coats fit many men," Elias murmured. "As do my rules."

"You don't have rules. You have appetites."

He laughed softly. "Tell me, Giselle—does Malcolm still pretend silence is a virtue? Or has he confessed the part where he kept me alive longer than I deserved?"

Her grip tightened on the receiver. "Try harder. You're fishing."

"Fishing?" His tone brightened. "I prefer netting. And you—" His breath lingered in the static. "You'll tire of this. Visibility is a performance diet. It eats muscle first."

"Watch me grow back," she snapped, and slammed the receiver down.

The silence that followed was jagged. Serena stared at her, eyes wide, then reached for the whiskey bottle and poured two fingers straight into her coffee. "Well," she said shakily, "he's got metaphors. Shame he's terrible at them."

Malcolm walked to the table and picked up the queen, turning it once in his hand before setting it back down carefully. His voice was low. "He wants you to believe exhaustion is the same as surrender."

"It isn't," Giselle said. Her hand still trembled, but her voice had steel. "We're not tired. We're awake."

Eva closed her laptop with a click. "Then tomorrow, we make sure the city wakes with us."

The room exhaled together. Outside, the city hummed, restless and waiting. Inside, the queen sat on the counter, ivory catching the dim light, no longer just a warning but a witness.

Chapter Twenty-Seven

Fire in the Glass

Morning came gray, with rain still clinging to the streets like a warning that hadn't burned off. Giselle hadn't closed her eyes. She'd spent the night staring at the faint scratch in the glass near her loft's window. Under certain light it looked like nothing. Under others it glimmered like a scar that might split wider at any second.

When Serena finally stirred, hair wild, socks mismatched, she caught Giselle at the window. "You've been staring at that thing all night," she muttered. "What are you expecting? It's not going to grow on command."

"I was waiting," Giselle said quietly.

"For what?"

"The glass to break."

Serena poured herself coffee and leaned against the counter. "That's not how physics works, G. But I get it. You think if you watch it long enough, you'll see the hand that left it."

"I don't have to see the hand," Giselle said. "I already know it belongs to them."

By nine, Eva arrived, fresh and sharp as if she had slept in a server room. She spread out a city map across the table. "Three safe sites scrubbed and ready," she said. "Coworking loft—neutral, cameras everywhere. A boutique hotel—solid locks, favors owed. And a church basement. Stone walls, no cameras, not on anyone's feed."

"Which has the best sight lines?" Malcolm asked from the window, his voice flat but awake.

"The hotel," Eva said.

"Then we don't take it," Giselle answered. "We take the basement. No one's watching saints."

Serena grinned despite the tension. "Finally, a holy war."

They packed quickly, leaving the loft immaculate, staged like a set they could weaponize. The queen remained on the sill, angled toward the street—a dare disguised as still life. Eva slid a sensor under the windowsill, a dime-sized node that would ping her laptop if the glass shifted even a hair. "If they touch it, I'll know," she said.

By eleven, they were in the basement of the old church, the fluorescents humming overhead like nervous witnesses. Folding chairs leaned against the wall, hymnals stacked in neat, dusty piles. Malcolm checked the exits, Serena wrestled a coffeemaker into service, Eva set up her screens like altars to truth. It wasn't glamorous, but it was safe enough.

At one, Eva's laptop beeped twice. She leaned forward, eyes narrowing. "Motion near your loft window. Two figures. Hooded."

"Feed?" Giselle asked, her throat tight.

Eva tapped. The grainy camera feed flickered to life: two men crouched on the rooftop across the street from her loft. One adjusted what looked like a tripod, the other held a small device glinting in the light.

"Laser mic," Eva said. "They're listening to silence."

"Amateurs," Serena muttered. "They're bored." She cracked her knuckles. "Let's give them static."

Eva keyed in a command. A low hum bled into the feed. The men adjusted their equipment, frowning. One pulled out a phone, snapped a picture of the loft window—the queen perched neatly in the frame.

Minutes later, social media buzzed. A new photo spread: *The Queen Still Watches.* The caption spawned hashtags. The watchers thought they had proof.

"Let them," Giselle said. "We own the inside."

At three, she went live from the basement, cinderblock walls stark behind her. She spoke directly into the camera, her face bare of makeup, her voice deliberate.

"You've seen images. A queen in a window. A scratch in glass. People want to make those things proof of something larger. But proof isn't in symbols. It's in voices. Tonight, survivors speak again. Don't mistake theater for truth."

She ended the stream. The comments poured in—supportive, skeptical, furious, enthralled. Confusion was armor, and she wore it well.

By evening, the basement filled. Folding chairs set in rows, cameras perched on tripods, survivors ready with trembling hands and clenched jaws. Serena moved through the space like a stage manager, Eva tuned the audio, Malcolm lingered at the back like a shadow stitched to the wall.

The first survivor, a retired teacher, stood and told her story—of trust misplaced, savings drained, silence bought with legal threats. Her voice shook, then steadied, and by the end her hands no longer trembled.

The second, a bartender, spoke sharper: of a partner who weaponized charm into debt, who left scars you couldn't photograph. Her story cracked the air like glass under pressure.

The third, a small business owner, gave numbers and dates like testimony, each one an indictment dressed as fact.

The room pulsed with their words. Giselle stood beside them, not in front, her presence amplifying rather than overshadowing.

Then her phone buzzed.

She almost ignored it. Then she slipped it from her pocket under the podium's shadow.

A photo.

Her loft window.

But now the glass was shattered, shards frozen mid-crash. The queen still sat on the sill, upright amid the wreckage.

Caption: *We break what you love, not what you bait.*

Her stomach knotted. She handed the phone to Malcolm. His jaw tightened, but he said nothing.

Eva scanned her feed, typing furiously. "No alarm," she said. "No sensor ping. That window isn't broken."

"They staged it," Serena spat. "Photoshopped, maybe smashed a copy. Either way, fake."

"They're inventing hauntings," Giselle said, forcing her voice calm.

"Then we prebunk again," Eva said. "Tomorrow morning, we release interior footage. Timestamped. Show the glass intact."

"Yes," Giselle said. Her voice grew steel. "We salt the earth before the lie can grow."

She turned back to the crowd, face smooth, voice unwavering. "Fear doesn't erase stories. It sharpens them. These voices you hear tonight are not fragile. They are precise. And precision cuts deeper than any threat."

The applause was quiet, reverent. The survivors exhaled like they'd been holding their breath for years.

Afterward, Serena pressed a cup of coffee into Giselle's hand. Eva muttered into her phone, already seeding the counter-story with friendly outlets. Malcolm stood at the door, eyes scanning every shadow.

The queen still sat in the loft window, unbroken, but the board around her was catching fire.

The queen still sat on her sill in the loft, unbroken. But the board around her was catching fire.

Chapter Twenty-Eight

The Glass Trap

Sleep never really arrived in the church basement. It lingered on the rafters like a bird that refused to land. Giselle lay on her cot with her coat drawn up to her collarbone, eyes fixed on the buzzing fluorescent lights. The queen was ten blocks away in her loft and ten feet high in her imagination, poised on the sill while shards of imaginary glass rained around it.

At five, she rose, brushed her hair into order, and brewed bitter coffee in the dented percolator Serena had bullied into working. Serena surfaced first, bleary but grinning. "Tell me there's cream or whiskey."

"Neither," Giselle said.

"Tragedy," Serena replied, and drank it black.

Malcolm emerged next, hair damp from splashing cold water on his face. He looked as though his body had rested but his mind had stood guard all night. Eva was last, though she appeared immaculate, eyeliner sharp, laptop already awake as if she'd been working in her sleep.

"Morning," Serena said. "What's burning?"

"Everything," Eva said briskly. "But the fake broken-window photo hasn't spread outside niche forums. We can starve it if we move now."

"Then let's starve it," Giselle said. "Walk me through today."

Malcolm leaned against the table, arms folded. "Two tracks. Public: you release timestamped footage of the loft—glass intact, queen unmoved. Surgical: we turn the loft into a stage they can't resist. Bait them in and catch them on record."

Serena grinned. "So, a party."

"A sting," Malcolm corrected.

Eva snapped her laptop shut. "I'll seed a rumor: you're hosting a photo shoot at the loft at noon. Candid candids. I'll add a second breadcrumb about a donor visit. Too tempting to ignore."

Giselle felt her pulse settle, the clarity that comes when fear becomes strategy. "Then we invite witnesses. Journalists, the councilwoman, the DA's office if they're brave. They'll expect us small. We'll give them an audience."

By eight, the nonprofit posted the footage: a slow 360 sweep of her loft, glass whole, queen upright. The timestamp glowed steady in the corner. Caption: *We don't live in your fictions.*

Comments split in two—some scoffing, some supportive—but the fake photo accounts went curiously silent.

At ten, their allies began to arrive at the loft. A trusted photographer with a canvas bag. Two journalists with the lean look of men who carried notebooks like shields. The councilwoman, spine sharp as glass. A plainclothes detective with posture like a locked door.

Giselle greeted them in the kitchen, voice steady. "House rules: no live posts, no premature narratives. You're witnesses, not stenographers. If this goes sideways, you testify because you were here, not because you wanted a headline."

They nodded. They understood the difference.

At eleven fifty-eight, Eva's feed caught the elevator pausing too long on Giselle's floor. Two men in maintenance coveralls loitered in the hallway, eyes too sharp for janitors.

"They're casing," Eva murmured.

Serena smoothed her hair like armor. "Good. Let's give them a show."

The first knock came at noon. Two short chimes on the bell, practiced politeness. Giselle pressed the intercom.

"Florist," a cheerful male voice said. "Delivery for Ms. Laurent."

Serena whispered, "I swear, if they bring another lily—"

Giselle opened the door an inch, chain still latched. A young man stood with a long white box, smile rehearsed. Behind him, another leaned against the wall, studying the reflection in a framed print.

"No flowers today," she said. "Try again never." She closed the door.

Thirty seconds later, the power flickered. The refrigerator sighed, the hallway camera winked out, then snapped back. Serena clapped once. "Cute. They think we didn't pay our bills."

Then came the long press of the bell. Malcolm checked the peephole and exhaled through his nose. "Preston."

Giselle undid the chain half an inch. Preston stood there in a crisp blue suit that wanted to impersonate authority. Bald Neck loomed behind him with a square white box. Farther back, the two "maintenance men" leaned against the wall, pretending disinterest.

"Quick word," Preston said smoothly.

"No," Giselle answered.

His eyes flicked past her shoulder, scanning the room. They landed on the queen in the window and his smile sharpened. "Some things belong to the board."

She closed the door in his face.

A moment later, three ritual knocks—tap, tap, tap. Silence. Tap, tap, tap again.

Giselle opened the door wide this time. The witnesses in the kitchen stood visible behind her. The councilwoman. The detective. Two cameras obviously filming.

"Invitation rescinded," she said. "But the audience is here if you'd like to perform."

Preston hesitated, then signaled to Bald Neck. The man lifted the lid of the box just enough to reveal rows of black-ribboned envelopes and a plastic queen gleaming cheap under the lights.

"Threats in bulk," Serena muttered. "Wholesale intimidation."

"Ceasefire," Preston said softly. "You take your queen off the sill. Go quiet. We walk away."

Giselle raised her phone and snapped a picture, making sure the detective's badge glinted in the frame. She sent it to Eva with a flick. "Extortion, documented."

Preston's jaw ticked. "Tonight it's photographs. Tomorrow it's medical bills."

The councilwoman's voice cracked like a whip. "That's witness intimidation, Mr. Preston. Say it out loud so the microphones catch it."

He blinked, recalibrated, then stepped back. "We're done."

He paused at the threshold, lowering his voice. "Queens wear crowns to hide scars."

"And pawns dream of promotion," Giselle replied evenly, closing the door.

The chain clicked home.

For a long moment the loft was silent, all of them listening to their own heartbeats. Then Serena let out a low whistle. "Well. That was dramatic."

Eva already had her laptop open again. "Upload complete," she said. "Prosecutors, reporters, three archivists. Preston just became a case study."

Malcolm checked the window, scanning the street. "He'll escalate."

"Yes," Giselle said. "But we'll be the ones choosing the board."

Chapter Twenty-Nine

Check and Countercheck

The theater smelled like dust and velvet and the last vows of a congregation that had moved on. Colored light from the stained glass freckled the empty seats; the stage boards creaked under Giselle's heels as if they recognized a woman who'd come to name things out loud. It felt right—half sacred, half staged. A room that could carry a confession without swallowing its speaker.

They built their scene fast. Eva staked out the wings with two laptops and a neat tangle of cables, all labeled in her sharp little handwriting. Serena lined water bottles on the edge of the stage like she was arming a choir. Malcolm took the aisles in long, quiet walks, counting exits, counting faces, counting the places a bad decision could enter.

Their witnesses arrived in a trickle that became a crowd: two journalists who made eye contact like a handshake, the civil-rights attorney with a voice that could sand a table smooth, the councilwoman whose spine looked like tempered glass, and a young prosecutor whose tie still shouted ambition. They sat where Serena pointed and stayed alert, as instructed—witnesses, not voyeurs.

"Too quiet," Serena murmured, sipping bad coffee. "Predators are never this polite."

"They're here," Malcolm said from the back, gaze slanting toward the double doors. "Two cars. Preston's in the lead."

Giselle centered herself on the boards and felt the room take her weight. "Raise the curtain," she said.

Preston arrived as if he owned aisles by birthright. Blue suit exact, expression laundered, Bald Neck half a step behind as if he intended to catch falling chandeliers with his shoulders. A third man trailed— new, blocky, watchful. Preston's smile reached for charm and found calculation.

"Ms. Laurent," he said, inventorying the councilwoman, the lawyer, the cameras. "You brought sunlight."

"You prefer attics," Giselle said. "We ran out."

His smile twitched. "Lovely venue. My compliments to your set designer."

"Consider it a rehearsal," Eva called from the wing, "for your deposition."

The journalists' pens scratched; the prosecutor's tie seemed to reconsider itself. Preston clasped his hands. "We're not here to fight. We're here to resolve."

"You offered resolution at my door," Giselle said. "It sounded like a bill."

"And yours sound like charity with cameras?"

"Receipts with dates," she said.

The attorney stepped forward, tone brisk. "You've been recorded threatening witnesses, interfering with communications, and delivering forged legal documents through intermediaries. You're out of verbs."

"Allegedly," Preston said, choosing his smile like a utensil.

"Repeatedly," Eva corrected, choosing the knife.

Before he could answer, the back doors sighed. A man entered alone.

He wore a gray coat that hung easy and expensive; his hood shadowed his face until he was halfway down the aisle. He didn't hurry. The room changed around him—the subtle shift people make when they think a name has just walked in wearing skin.

He lifted his hood.

The resemblance hit like a camera flash: the lean, clever face; the eyes brighter than they needed to be; the smile that pretended warmth until you looked long enough to see angles. Not perfect—older maybe, or different at the edges—but grief is elastic, and memory slips its leash when it wants to believe.

Malcolm stiffened. His breath left him in a sound almost too small to hear. "Don't," he breathed, but to whom he said it—Giselle, himself, the room—wasn't clear.

The man's gaze found him. "Little brother," he said, soft, intimate, pitched to carry without seeming to try.

It was the voice that did it for Malcolm at first—a timbre that reached into a cupboard only the two of them knew. But it was the hand that made his face drain: as the man lifted a casual palm, Giselle saw it too—the crescent scar on the ring-finger knuckle, pale against tan skin. A shallow half-moon like a healed bite.

Malcolm spoke without taking his eyes off it. "Bike chain," he said hoarsely. "We were kids. He tried to jump the curb, the chain bit him, and he laughed while he bled—said pain meant he'd earned the ride."

The man's smile warmed, almost fond. "You remember," he said.

Giselle felt the room lean toward belief and forced it back with a breath. Makeup can fake a scar. A decoy can be taught a brother's history. "Names are costumes," she told him. "Which one are you wearing today?"

"You may call me Elias," he said lightly.

The councilwoman didn't smile. "We may," she said. "And we may not."

He ignored her and shifted his attention to Giselle as if they were alone. "You've built an audience," he said. "Imagine what you could build with mine. Power is choreography. Visibility is currency. Keep your stage. I'll keep my ledgers. Together, we write the show. You'd stop fighting for scraps of light and start selling the sun."

He sold worship disguised as partnership, cuffs disguised as bracelets, a future that sounded like surrender with better lighting.

Giselle let the pitch breathe just long enough to hear how empty it rang, then clicked play on the recorder in her hand. His voice from the landline—the call after the vigil—filled the theater: You've mistaken yourself for a director. You could be more than a queen. You could be the whole game.

The echo rang off stained glass. The journalists' pens accelerated. The attorney's smile acquired edges. Preston's jaw turned to geometry.

The man in gray laughed, indulgent. "A parlor trick," he said.

Eva, without looking up, slid a stamped folder to the attorney. "Chain of custody," she said. "Three witnesses to receipt. Two to transfer. Timecode on original inbound."

The councilwoman's voice cut like glass. "You are less myth by the minute."

A flicker crossed his face—annoyance, maybe, or the surprise of a magician whose audience knows how sleeves work. He turned back to Malcolm, softening again. "You could come home."

Malcolm's gaze dropped to the scar, then climbed back to the man's eyes. His voice steadied. "I did," he said. "It just isn't yours."

The sentence landed with a clean weight. The man's expression faltered for the first time—no drama, just the smallest crack where certainty had lived.

Preston stepped in as if to salvage momentum. "Here's the deal," he said briskly. "You stand down. Take your queen off the sill. No more speeches, no more docks, no more hotel doorways. You go quiet, and this… confusion… resolves."

"No," Giselle said, and felt the word resonate through wood. "We choose the board now."

Preston's mouth tightened. He made a tiny motion with two fingers; Bald Neck shifted his stance like a punctuation mark. The young prosecutor glanced at the councilwoman, who tilted her chin almost imperceptibly: steady.

The man in gray considered the audience—councilwoman, attorney, cameras, lights—then Giselle again, as if studying a painting he meant to steal. He lifted his hand casually, and there it was a second time: the crescent scar, unmistakable in its place.

He said, almost idly, "Queens don't leave the file. They take the diagonal."

Malcolm flinched so slightly only Giselle felt it. That was a line from their childhood chess lessons—Elias's private mantra when he coached a bolder move than the board seemed to allow. Not famous. Not printed anywhere. A phrase you'd only know if you were there.

Or if you'd been taught to say it.

Giselle didn't cede the frame. "And pawns don't dream," she said evenly. "They evolve."

"Sometimes they break," he offered.

"Sometimes they arrive," she returned.

He watched her, then smiled with something like reluctant admiration. "Careful," he murmured. "Houses of glass look like churches until stones remember gravity."

"And men who throw them forget cameras exist," she said.

Preston cleared his throat, rescued by bureaucracy. "We'll be in touch," he said stiffly.

The man in gray lingered a beat, gaze sliding to Malcolm with that same private brightness. Then he turned and walked up the aisle, not fast, not slow, coat moving like a curtain. Preston followed; Bald Neck last, giving the stage a stare that mistook mass for power.

The doors sighed shut. The room exhaled.

For a moment no one spoke. The colored light lay across the stage like confetti after a parade. Serena let out a breath that sounded too loud in the sudden quiet. "Okay," she said. "That was either him or the best community-theater performance this city has seen."

The attorney tucked the folder against her chest. "Doesn't matter. We got what we needed." She turned to Giselle. "You have more friends than you think."

Eva sealed an evidence bag around the recorder, her hands precise. "Three angles, clean audio, two public officials on premises," she said. "If they try to cut around this, they'll bleed continuity."

The young prosecutor loosened his tie like a man who had just survived a baptism. "My office will call before noon," he promised the room, which everyone pretended meant just Giselle.

Giselle nodded without really seeing him. Her eyes had found Malcolm in the footlights. He was watching his hands, as if the scar had been transferred there and might confess under inspection.

"You keep going," he said finally, looking up. The quiet in him wasn't emptiness; it was a decision. "I keep going with you."

For a heartbeat the theater felt like a church again—not the hush of fear but the hum of chosen allegiance. Giselle swallowed down the ache that always came when she realized she wasn't alone.

"Good," she said. "Because it's not checkmate. It's check and countercheck. He moves; we move back. But from now on, we choose the board."

Serena bumped her shoulder. "And we choose fries."

"Fries," Giselle agreed, because ritual is a strategy, too.

The councilwoman squeezed her forearm in passing, a pressure that felt like a vote. The attorney gave a small nod that a different kind of courtroom would recognize. The journalists slid their notebooks into bags like they were sheathing knives. Eva shut the last laptop. Malcolm took one last slow look at the exits, as if asking them politely to remain doors.

They left the theater together, not rushing, the way people leave rooms they own at least for a night. Outside, the city's evening was blue and unbothered. Inside Giselle's chest, something that had been braced finally unclenched—then braced again when she saw the memory in Malcolm's face: the crescent scar, the private line, the way belief and doubt could stand shoulder to shoulder and both feel like truth.

"Tomorrow," she said softly as they reached the door, speaking to him and to the room and to the stained glass that had watched them all, "we move the board."

He nodded. "Tomorrow."

And the theater, empty now of men who believed light belonged to them, kept their echoes like an affidavit.

Chapter Thirty

Endgame

The theater exhaled them into the city night like a final bow. Outside, neon buzzed, tires hissed on wet asphalt, strangers hurried past without knowing a stage had just hosted a war. Giselle pulled her coat tighter, not against the cold but against the weight of what had been said and what had been seen. For the first time in weeks, witnesses outnumbered shadows. That was victory, however fragile.

They walked in silence until Serena broke it. "I don't know about you," she said, heels clicking, "but I just argued with the devil in stained glass. That earns me fries."

"Fries," Giselle echoed, and the group smiled for the first time that day.

The chrome diner down the block gleamed like a time capsule. Booths squeaked, jukebox hummed, coffee smelled of burnt beans and stubbornness. The waitress called them sweethearts and brought four baskets without asking. They ate in the easy noise of grease and neon, ritual cushioning the shock of theater.

"You realize," Serena said around a fry, "we just invented a support group where carbs are therapy."

"Better than silence," Malcolm said.

The words hung heavier than he intended. His eyes were distant, locked on something she couldn't see. The scar. The phrase. The possibility that Elias wasn't dead at all—or worse, that someone had taught another man how to wear his history.

Giselle nudged his foot under the table, grounding him. "Better than silence," she agreed.

Eva never paused typing, fries cooling at her elbow. "Files are already seeded. Three outlets, two prosecutors, one archive. Preston and his men will be lawyering up by breakfast. Their myth is cracked, whether Elias himself walks or not."

"And if he does?" Serena asked.

"Then he walks into discovery," Eva replied, voice like sharpened steel.

Back at the loft, the queen still perched on the sill, outward-facing, daring the night. The loft looked staged, a diorama waiting for predators to misread it. Giselle touched the back of the queen lightly, then left it there.

They were all bone-tired, but adrenaline still burned under their skin. When the knock came—three deliberate raps—none of them startled.

Malcolm opened the door an inch. Two men stood in the hall, new faces, but with the same flat posture of men who delivered messages without return addresses. One wore a cap low; the other was taller, silent.

"Ms. Laurent," Cap said, voice polite, almost weary. "You're needed."

"By whom?" Eva asked, already raising her phone.

"By sense," Cap said. "By safety. Come with us."

"That's not an answer," Serena cut in. "That's a Sudoku puzzle."

Giselle stepped forward, meeting his gaze. "If your employer wants me, he can knock in daylight with a name and a badge. Otherwise, he sends delivery boys who don't even tip."

Cap's eyes flicked over her shoulder to the queen in the window. "You're playing a dangerous game."

"I don't play," she said. "I rewrite."

For a moment, the four of them and the two of them stood still, the hallway holding its breath. Then Cap nodded once. "You'll hear from us."

Eva's tone was ice. "We already did."

The men withdrew without turning their backs, swallowed by the elevator's ding.

Silence rushed in, heavy as water. Giselle braced her hand on the counter. "He's not finished."

"No," Malcolm said, jaw tight. "But neither are we."

Eva snapped her laptop shut. "Everything is live now. They'll spend the week swatting subpoenas. Their myth won't feed them anymore."

"Not unless he's real," Serena said quietly.

The words landed sharp. All eyes turned, unspoken memories rising: the scar, the chess phrase, the way Malcolm's voice had cracked when he saw the man in gray.

Malcolm finally spoke, each word deliberate. "I knew that scar. I knew that line. If it wasn't him, then someone studied him the way you study scripture."

Giselle's throat tightened. "Or he's alive."

Silence answered. None of them liked the weight of either option.

Her phone buzzed against the counter. Unknown number. A photo this time: a slip of paper, handwriting sharp and angled. She knew it before she even showed it to Malcolm.

Queens don't leave the file.

The same phrase the man had murmured in the theater. Elias's private coaching line, a mantra Malcolm had once repeated at kitchen tables when they were boys.

Malcolm's face hardened. "That's him. No one else knows that."

"Unless he taught them," Eva said evenly.

"Or left enough behind for someone to study," Serena added, though even she sounded unconvinced.

Giselle forced her hand steady, thumbed a reply: *Queens arrive. And witnesses watch.*

She hit send.

She walked to the window, lifted the queen from the sill, and set it down on the chessboard in the middle of the table. For weeks it had been a warning. Tonight, it was her choice.

"End of act," she whispered.

The queen gleamed under lamplight. The note still glowed on her phone.

And somewhere in the city, a man—alive or perfectly imitated—was smiling.

The Quiet Between Moves

Morning sunlight crept through the blinds in uneven stripes, cutting across the loft like bars. Giselle sat at the table in her robe, a half-empty mug cooling at her elbow, the queen on the chessboard where she'd left it the night before. For weeks it had been bait. Now it was hers.

Serena shuffled in wearing mismatched socks and a T-shirt that threatened to disintegrate. She yawned loudly, then eyed the queen. "So we've upgraded from window decoration to centerpiece?"

Giselle smiled faintly. "Better to choose where it stands than let them."

"Fair," Serena said, pouring coffee that tasted more like rust than beans. She slid into the chair across from her. "So. End of act. Do we get an intermission, or do we just keep playing?"

"Both," Giselle said.

The knock came softer this time, just one tap. Malcolm entered, freshly showered but with eyes that hadn't slept. He carried an old wallet in his hand. From it, he pulled a yellowed scrap of paper—the handwriting faded but still sharp. He set it on the table between them.

Giselle recognized it instantly. The same hand as the note on her phone the night before. The same angular A's, the same stabbing cuts at the tops of letters.

Malcolm's voice was low. "I kept this from when we were kids. His handwriting never changed. Whoever wrote you last night—it was him."

Eva arrived next, crisp as ever, laptop already open. She glanced at the scrap but didn't touch it. "Handwriting can be forged," she said. "But the scar, the phrase, the letters… if this is a forgery, it's someone with access no one should have."

Serena leaned back, blowing on her coffee. "So either Elias crawled out of the grave, or he left a manual behind and someone's reading it like scripture. Neither option is my favorite."

No one laughed.

Giselle reached across the table and moved the queen two squares forward. The sound of ivory on wood was louder than it should have been. "I don't need to know which yet. I just need to know he's still watching. And that means he's still worried."

"Or planning," Malcolm said.

"Then we plan louder," Giselle replied.

Eva finally looked up from her screen. "The city believes he's alive now. Some are terrified, some emboldened. That's dangerous."

"That's leverage," Giselle said. "Fear makes people listen. We'll decide what they hear."

For a long moment, none of them spoke. The loft hummed with the low thrum of the refrigerator, the far-off buzz of traffic, the faint pulse of a city waking up. Giselle's phone buzzed once on the counter. She didn't move to check it. Not yet.

Malcolm rested his hand on the back of her chair. His voice carried no comfort, only truth. "He's out there."

"Or someone wants us to believe he is," Giselle said. She tapped the queen lightly, her eyes steady. "Either way, we don't wait for the next move. We set the board."

Serena raised her mug. "To the quiet between moves," she said.

Eva didn't raise hers, but her fingers stilled on the keyboard—a rare gesture of agreement.

Giselle lifted her cup last, the queen gleaming on the board between them. "To the next act," she said softly.

And outside, the city stirred, restless and listening.

About the Author

Gladys Stocks is a resilient and inspiring author. In 2007, she tragically lost her three-year-old son as a result of being in an abusive relationship. For 16 years, she grappled with guilt and grief, but in 2023, she channeled her pain into writing her first novella, "NEVER WOULD HAVE MADE IT: How Overcoming Grief and Loss Saved My Life," to help others suffering in silence.

She founded "Just Love Self," a brand dedicated to encouraging women to love themselves unapologetically, offering homemade gifts and promoting self-care through her, "The Self Love Challenge: 30 Day Challenge to a Better You" Workbook and Coloring Book. Despite the challenges of dealing with anxiety, depression, and the loss of her son, Gladys has become a beacon of hope and resilience, inspiring others to overcome adversity and cherish self-love and mental health.